BORN IN DARKNESS

MAFIA ELITE, BOOK 3

AMY MCKINLEY

ARROWSCOPE PRESS, LLC

Born in Darkness

Copyright © 2021 Amy McKinley

(p) **ISBN**-13: 978-1-951919-14-6

(e) **ISBN**-13: 978-1-951919-13-9

Publisher: Arrowscope Press, LLC; www.arrowscopepress.com

Editing— Kate Birdsall, Line Editor, Taylor Anhalt, Proofreader, Red Adept Editing

Cover Design—T.E. Black Designs; www.teblackdesigns.com

Author photo provided by—Brookelyn Anhalt of lovely.life.photography; https://www.facebook.com/LovelyLifePhotography-102253596490708

Interior Formatting & Design— Arrowscope Press, LLC; www.arrowscopepress.com

THE FAMILY

**Chicago Outfit
Italian American Mafia**

Caruso Family
Antonio – (father, former boss, deceased)
Maria (first wife, deceased, Max's Mom)
Nicole (second wife (Tony's Mom, Elena's adopted Mom))
Tony (son)
Maximus "Max" (son, boss)
Elena (adopted daughter)
Vito (advisor to boss)
Maria's family from Italy
Salvio "Sal" (cousin)
Cristiano (cousin)
Tommasso (cousin)
Aunt Rosa (lives in Sicily)

Brambilla Family
Benito (former boss, deceased)

Julia (wife, deceased)
Liliana "Lil" (daughter)
Leonardo (underboss, cousin)
Dino (advisor to boss)
Eva (cousin)
Vincenzo (Julia's Sicilian father, Liliana's grandfather)

La Rosa Family
Robert (boss)
Angela (wife)
Marco (son, underboss)
Nico (son)
Trey (son)
Sofia (daughter)
Maso (boss's brother, advisor)
Tom (captain)

Vitale Family
Emilio (boss)
Alessia (wife)
Enzo (son, underboss)
Emiliana "Em" (daughter)
Aldo (advisor to boss)
Renato "Ren" (captain)

Rossi Family
Frank (father, boss)
Carla (mother, deceased)
Camila (daughter)
Stefano (son, underboss)
Alfonso (son, deceased)
Marissa (daughter, deceased)
Drago (advisor to the boss)

Russian Mafia
Pavlov Bratva

Pavlov Bratva
Yuri (boss)
Mischa (wife)
Ivan (eldest son, former underboss, deceased)
Victor "Vic" (son, underboss)
Katya (angel of death, assassin)

CHAPTER ONE

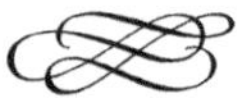

STEFANO

I stopped in front of my childhood home, pulling the damp, icy chill of the morning into my lungs as I stared at that overbearing tower of bricks. The longer I stood there, the more I swore I could smell the alcoholic fumes that had permeated my mother's breath every damned day of my childhood. Mom had turned to drinking to escape the monster she'd married. Unfortunately, she'd left me and my siblings to deal with reality —and *him*. And then she'd left us altogether.

I was the last kid standing—our last chance at revenge.

My father's days as head of the Rossi Chicago Mafia family were numbered. He just hadn't realized it yet. And he sure as hell had no idea who would be ushering in his demise.

Me.

With no more time to waste, I strode up the concrete pavers that led to that cold, three-story mansion. I nodded at the made men, the soldiers we'd stationed at the pillars as I passed, then pushed my way through the heavy double doors.

I rubbed my jaw, working to ease the ache from clenching my teeth as I crossed the foyer to the scarred wood beneath the second-floor balcony. Mom had died five years ago today.

toed the area that looked like it was still stained with her blood.

My mind traveled back to that fateful day. As the horror of those last few moments of Mom's life washed over me, I closed my eyes and let them play like a movie through my mind.

My youngest sister and I had been reeling after learning that Camila, the oldest of what used to be the four of us, had left for Russia that morning. An arranged marriage contract had been signed between our family and the Pavlov Bratva. Our father had kept the details to himself then sprung her departure on my mom, sisters, and me.

We'd had a matter of minutes to acclimate to the idea of her leaving—to join the enemy—and then she was gone.

Mom hadn't compartmentalized the departure, the loss, of her firstborn as well as Marissa and I had. Later that afternoon, we heard glass shatter in the foyer, and Marissa and I cautiously crept toward the sound to investigate. An empty bottle of vodka, Mom's drink of choice, lay in pieces on the wood floor. Dad was by the front door, while Mom was at the top of the landing. I could still hear her screams as she railed at him.

"You sent my daughter to her death!" Tears streamed down Mom's face as she wavered back and forth.

"I handled a business problem. She happened to be the price owed, and she did her duty with more grace than you're showing." His disgust was clear in the scowl on his face.

Marissa clasped my hand, and I tugged her back so that we were hidden in the shadows, not that I had any doubt that Dad was aware we were there. But I couldn't leave, and neither could she, because we both knew that hellish day was far from over.

Camila was one year older than me and had four on Marissa, who would enter college as a freshman after the summer. Dad hadn't even let Camila graduate before marrying her off.

"I hate you." Mom's hands gripped the railing, her hair curtaining her grief-stricken face.

"You're emotional and drunk. When you're sober and in the right frame of mind to have this conversation, come find me." My father dismissed her and headed down the hallway to his office.

A wounded scream made both Marissa and me press harder against the wall. I clenched my fists as dread crawled along my spine. Mom dragged a chair over, sobbing the entire time as we stood frozen, afraid to move or console her—not when she'd been drinking. It never ended well. Camila had been her favorite and the only one who could talk her out of her drunken insanity.

I tracked Mom's movements as she wobbled while standing on the chair. Then she placed a bare foot on the railing, and I jerked forward, unable to remain a quiet observer any longer. "No!"

All my shout did was still her trembling form, and her unfocused gaze landed on Marissa and me. With a shake of her head, she whispered the clearest words I'd heard from her in months. "I can't anymore. I hate him, and I will not witness what he'll do to you two." She shook her head. "I can't."

Mom transferred her weight to the foot perched on the banister then launched herself headfirst over it. There was a buzzing in my ears as time slowed, and I watched with horror as her head struck the ground where the pieces of glass were, embedding themselves into both the wood and her skull. Her body crumpled on impact. My feet felt encased in cement. Eventually, the buzzing registered as coming from Marissa, who was on her knees, screaming.

"There is no room in this life for sentimentality." My father's cigar-roughened voice pierced the haze of memory and yanked me back to the present with a resounding snap.

I said nothing. If I had, he would have used it against me. I was the last one remaining, and even though he would never admit it, he needed me, if only from the standpoint of projecting the illusion of strength against all others. His cold gaze dropped to the scarred wood I'd been staring at, and he smirked as I watched him from the corner of my eye.

"Thinking of the night your mom jumped?" He shook his head. "She was weak, just like the rest of them. As for you? I'm still waiting to see if you have the potential and the fortitude the rest lacked." He pointed his cigar at me. "But regardless whether you amount to more, you'll always be my second, never good enough to lead."

I raised my gaze from where we'd both fixated, determination and hatred building to almost overflowing. Mom might have committed suicide, but the bastard she'd married had murdered her all the same. I kept my voice dispassionate, knowing that he would drop a verbal bomb. He always did. I braced for it. "Is that so?"

"It is. You're my shield. Expendable. Each of you had a purpose."

"Alfonso did?" I raised a brow in challenge. He had been seven years old when he was shot and killed in the park because he'd been in the way of the bullet meant for Elena. *What could his purpose have been?*

"If he'd lived, he would have. I had two sons for a situation like that."

He was a sick bastard. None of us mattered. Mom's job was to bear him children that would equal power when he bartered us in whatever business deal suited him best. I'd played his game long enough to know how he worked.

I held still. He wasn't done dispelling his words of wisdom.

"Know this. If there is anything that takes your focus away from what I require of you—and don't think I haven't noticed your interest in Emiliana Vitale—I'll eliminate those distractions."

The familiar rage hissed inside of me. I would not react. My muscles locked down, keeping me from attacking him and ending his miserable existence. I made no move, showed no emotion. He studied me, searching. He would find no reaction. I wouldn't allow it.

Another second or two passed before he grunted then pivoted on his heel and headed in the direction of his office. I didn't move or break my mask until I was sure he was gone. It wasn't the first time he'd threatened Emiliana. He'd done the same a little over four years prior, a few weeks before she'd disappeared. I hadn't been able to prove it, but I feared he'd had something to do with the human trafficking ring that had taken her.

I'd gotten her back, but it should never have happened. Somehow, I would find a way to link my father, the Rossi boss, to the worst experience in her life and then end him, giving her, my sisters, my brother, and my mother the vengeance they all deserved.

I peered down the dark hallway after him. "I'm made of stronger stuff than you." Under my breath, I voiced what would happen, what my legacy was. "Beware, old man. You'll never see me coming."

CHAPTER TWO

EMILIANA

Sleep hadn't come easy. I tossed and turned, plagued by past horrors. The sheets twisted around my legs, holding me prisoner. I wanted to wake up, to escape the images that came to life behind closed eyes. My groggy mind wouldn't allow me to surface—awakening memories that were better left buried.

Everything hurt. Bruises marred my body. My face throbbed and ached in tune with the erratic beat of my pulse. I'd hurt my captors back, refusing to lay still, to be complacent. Even when terror seeped into my bones, I remembered who I was. The blood running through my veins was of stronger stuff than they ever would be. I chose to fight. They were dead men walking.

Loud pops followed by screams removed the man responsible for the condition of my swelling face. Inside, I laughed. Death was coming, and it wasn't for me. Weighted down by atrophying muscles too long in restraints, my limbs didn't comply when I tried tugged on my bindings, desperate to help whoever had found me.

For so long, a mantra ran on repeat in my mind, one that'd finally happened—my family had come. My ears strained as I lay tethered on the dirty mattress. Was it my brother? I expected it to be him.

Enzo would never stop searching from the moment I was taken. I'd just had to hold out, stay alive. And not let fear and despair consume me. It'd been damn hard. There were moments… but I lived. I was here.

The gunshots were closer. Bodies fell to the ground, each one satisfying the darkest part of me that demanded revenge. Screams penetrated my ears, chasing more of the haziness in my thoughts away. Then I heard him calling my name.

Stefano. An underboss for the Rossi family, and the only one I'd ever had feelings for. And he was close. More gunfire exploded not far, and I tried to shout to him, to tell him I was here.

The door to my room, or cell, crashed open. Tall and muscular, he filled the doorway. An avenging angel with his dark-blond hair and eyes that promised death. When he reached for me, I gasped awake, thrown from the nightmare and into the present.

I tore the sheets from my body and gulped air. Flinging the covers back, I hurried into the bathroom and splashed water on my face.

My path was chosen the day I was born then set in stone when they took me. I dried my face then returned to my bedroom where I picked up my phone, turned it on, and pulled up the photo I kept hidden from the entire world—but especially my dad.

Stefano. My heart clenched as his intense gaze stared up at me. The man I was forbidden to love. And yet, he was the one man I did love. That I'd always loved. While my family was fine with my older—and only—brother, Enzo, interacting with him, they'd warned me when they noticed my interest early on that nothing could ever come of it. Therefore, my attraction needed to die a quick death.

Only, it never did. It grew instead, at least until the day when

I was abducted and everything changed. My obsession with him hadn't ended, but my freedom had.

I tossed my phone onto the bed and shoved my hands through my hair, and wandered into my walk-in closet. I needed to do something by myself, just because I could. I didn't need to have my friends or family with me twenty-four seven.

I'd clawed my way through hell and emerged… changed. I was the last one of my friends who was still single and clinging to it. But lately, something inside me had shifted, altered—again.

I loved my family. They were incredible. We were Mafia royalty, and the life wasn't easy, but they were always there for me. Not all of us had that, growing up. As usual, Stefano swam to the forefront of my mind. I used to be wary of him and of who he came from, despite how drawn I was to him. His father was cold and uncaring, ruthless. His family had been riddled by tragedy—so much death. His brother, mother, and sister, who had been one of my closest friends, were all dead. And rather than cherishing the children he had left, Frank Rossi had married his oldest daughter to the enemy, the Russians, and treated his only living son, Stefano, as the dirt beneath his shoes.

For as long as I'd known him, Stefano's gaze would scan the room—my guess was to note the exits. His responses were curt and his body language tense, as if ready to fight, and there had been a time in my long crush when I was cautious of him. That was until he saved me, literally carrying me out of hell. Now, he consumed my thoughts. And even though I portrayed a tough, vicious outer exterior, inside, I was afraid. I'd convinced everyone except for Stefano. He saw inside me in a way few did.

Times were changing, and I wasn't sure where I fit. My best friends, Lil and Sofia, were preoccupied with their relationships. Eva, Lil's cousin, was in our group, too, but she came across as an annoying gnat to me more often than not.

I took one last look in the floor-length mirror to make sure my weapons were out of sight before leaving to go to the coffee place not far from our house with a book. I narrowed my eyes as I swept over my outfit, a red cashmere sweater with a deep V-neck that matched the color of my lipstick and deadly black pants Sofia had made that contained many hidden weapons, including several knives and a choke wire. Rings adorned my fingers and would hurt like hell if I needed to punch anyone. In my oversized purse was my 9mm and an extra magazine. I dropped my phone inside, aware that the finder app that gave my location to Enzo was on. It was the only way my brother was even remotely okay with me leaving the house without him.

Next were the teardrop diamond earrings Stefano had given me, with a location device hidden in them as well. Prior to my abduction, I would have been pissed about having a tracker on me, but things had changed. I trusted my family to keep me safe. And Stefano embodied the darkness. But where he had been terrifying before, he'd become my savior. Besides, I preferred the monster to the white knight. The monster would slay all my dragons and scare our enemies too.

I grabbed my iPad with the book I planned to read and forced myself to leave my room. Each time was challenging, as fear crawled over my skin in a cold sweat. But I had to go. I wouldn't allow my experience in hell to make me a prisoner.

As I crossed the threshold from my room to the hall, I sensed the first barrier. *I'm stronger than my anxiety.* I made my way down the stairs and out the front door to my waiting Mercedes S-Class Guard, another concession to my brother, as the car was basically armored and I insisted on going out without my guards… at least, I liked to pretend they weren't with me, but they always were, just not in the same car as me. I'd put my foot down about that. I wanted to be in control, and I would drive myself.

It didn't take long to get to The Coffee Stop, and I parked close to the front door on the street. An entourage of black cars containing my guards followed me. I didn't wait for them but got out and headed inside. My family knew I was going out, and soon, so would Stefano. I glanced at the time. I would have a few minutes at most until he arrived, if he was able to break away from whatever he was doing. Either way, I silently repeated the mantra I told myself every time I went somewhere outside of the house: *I will be fine.*

I ordered my coffee with my purse unzipped, allowing easy access to my gun in case I needed it. I wouldn't, but it made me feel better. I sometimes went out with it in hand but flush against my leg, only when I couldn't make myself leave the house any other way. Good thing we owned the place, and the employees were used to me.

Coffee in hand, I found where I wanted to sit. My back was to the wall, and I had the perfect view of the front door and the hallway that led to the restrooms. Plants surrounded the table on either side, offering enough privacy but not hindering my sightline of the two places I needed to be aware of to be somewhat comfortable.

I settled into an armchair that my brother had placed precisely, along with a reserved sign on the table so it would always be available when I came in. The staff had strict instructions to keep any customers out of my spot.

Part of getting better was training in the room Enzo designed for me and also leaving the house on my own. Going to meet my friends was no problem, but I struggled to relax when alone. I was on high alert. I pulled out my phone and set the timer for an hour. I would force myself to stay until it went off.

I pulled the Kindle app up on my iPad and found the book I was reading, a hilarious contemporary romance. No way would

I entertain the romantic suspense or thriller I'd downloaded the day before. I could only devour those in the safety of my home, where I wouldn't fall into a panic at every little thing. *This sucks. I want to be like I used to be, completely fearless.*

With a sigh, I adjusted the iPad's stand and got comfortable. It didn't take long until a grin teased the corners of my mouth, and I lost track of time. The author was hilarious, and I loved how the characters interacted. After a few sips of coffee, I was absorbed in the book's storyline—until a sudden noise forced me back to reality.

The bells above the door jingled, and I tightened my grip on the iPad, ready to use it as a weapon. I tracked the two people who'd entered. Once they'd ordered and taken their seat far enough from me, I took a deep breath, releasing the tightness that had locked up my muscles. Once I loosened my hold on my device, the anxiety of an ambush gone, I dropped my gaze back to the story. It took a few tries to sink back into the fiction world, but I kept trying.

Then I got to the first kissing scene, and my heart rate increased. It was a great scene, but I had one in my mind that was so much better. Not my first, but just as good. I let my mind skip back to about a year before the getting-abducted-in-Italy incident. I had been in my last year of high school and was wandering around the Rossis' house, pretending to look for another bathroom, as Sofia was in the one attached to Marissa's room. The truth was, I wanted to find Stefano.

And I found him. From under my lashes, I glanced at Stefano. It was a subtle move. I tried to keep the need I felt in his presence hidden, but we were alone in the hallway. Power crackled around him, and I shivered at the strength emanating from his imposing presence. It was something that had always drawn me to him—that and how kind he was to his sisters.

The opportunity to be alone with Stefano was rare, and I

would not have let that one slip away because I was shy or nervous. I lifted my chin and let everything I was feeling—desire, attraction, sheer need—show on my face. Something dark flared in his eyes, and my lips parted.

Then I was in his arms, my back against the wall as his lips devoured mine in a soul-searing kiss. I lost myself to the decadence of his mouth moving over mine, the teasing caress of his tongue, and the way his arms sheltered me in his embrace. Heat built through my body, tiny explosions of desire as he deepened the kiss.

His hand cupped the back of my neck, tangling in my long hair. The gentle tug on the strands only increased my need for him. I arched against his hard body, encouraging him to take more, longing to feel skin against skin.

I ran my hands over his shoulders, reveling in the way his muscles rippled beneath my fingertips. The steel band of his arm around my waist shifted until he palmed my ass. With slight pressure, he lifted me. I wound my legs around him, groaning when I felt his hard length at the apex of my thighs. Heat pooled in my core, and I ground against him. When he moaned, a shiver raced over my spine.

Threading my fingers through his hair, I pressed impossibly closer, tangling my tongue with his, blind in my need. A noise pierced the haze of desire. Stefano tore his lips from mine, and I whimpered, unable to hold in the disappointment. He jerked back then quickly untangled my legs, helping me to slide down his amazingly solid body. I was slow to react—he felt too sinfully good.

Once I was back on my feet, unsteady but standing, he tugged me with him. We rushed toward the bathroom, where he'd been leaving and I'd been headed. He pulled me inside then shut and locked the door. I leaned against it as my heart rate slowly returned to normal.

When the haze of lust dissipated, I saw his expression clearly. Remorse pulled the corners of his lips down, and I growled. I knew what was coming.

He raked his hands through his hair. "I'm sorry, Em. I didn't mean to attack you in the hallway." He turned away, pacing the length of the bathroom. "Fuck."

The last of the haze burned off at his words. "I'm not fragile." I grabbed his arm and tugged him to me so that our eyes met and held. "I wanted that and more. Stop acting like I'll break. If I don't want you to do something, I'll tell you."

The sound of my phone's alarm jarred me, and my gaze darted around the dimly lit interior of The Coffee Stop. There were a few people at the tables, talking but not doing anything out of the ordinary. My heart rate slowed to normal, and I smiled because I had done it. I made it without panic attacks. Not only that, but I didn't want to leave. So I didn't.

Another hour passed, and I read several more chapters until I was ready to go. It was nearing lunch, and I wanted to try out a new recipe I'd found. My iPad went back into my purse and the to-go coffee cup in the trash before I wound through the tables with more confidence in my step than I'd had in a very long time. The bell jingled overhead as I pushed through the door and exited onto the sidewalk outside.

I'd parked almost directly in front and hesitated to go to my car. I was feeling great and not quite ready to go home. Unusual, but I was going with it. My guards trailed me as I turned right rather than left to get into my car.

It was fall, my favorite season, and there was no hurry to get home. I hadn't told my brother where I was going because he and Sofia had recently returned from Italy, engaged. I was thrilled for them, especially given all they'd had to endure over the past few years. They'd found their way back to one another and needed their space. They even had their own house, and I wasn't going to ruin that.

Pushing their very tangible happiness from my thoughts, I focused on my surroundings and window-shopped. I passed by my favorite boutique and paused. Sofia needed to open up a store like it and sell her designs. I would bring that up with her soon. With the idea lodged in my mind to tell her the next time I saw her, I moved farther down the sidewalk.

A cool breeze whipped down the street, blowing my long hair behind me, and I lifted my face to the crisp air, looking forward to sitting around a fire with a blanket and mug of coffee. My parents were out of town, and I was the only one in the house. It was strange but also good for me, as it had been over four years since the incident. I'd leaned on my family and friends for the past few years, working through PTSD from being abducted. I had good coping mechanisms in place, even if my go-to method was violence. That was to be expected, though, and something I was fine with, as was my family.

Ensuring enough distance between other people and myself, I noted the pedestrians hurrying into stores or work, and I felt… free. It wasn't often that the past didn't have a choke hold on me, and I'd learned to enjoy every second of it when it didn't. Thankfully, those times were becoming more frequent.

There was an Italian deli not far ahead, and I wanted to stop in and browse. I didn't think I had any good prosciutto for the recipe I wanted to make for lunch. My hand closed around the door handle, and I started to pull it open when someone clamped onto my arm from behind.

Everything slowed. I could count each breath from the time I felt the touch to the tension increasing as whoever it was attempted to turn me. I went with it, releasing my grasp on the door and flicking my wrist so a knife dropped into my hand. My heart thudded in my ears. Within a second, he was within sight. Tall, dusty blond hair, and a smile that portrayed his interest—but I wasn't.

"Let go," I growled, clutching the knife against my side.

A flash of something I didn't like lit in his eyes, and his grip tightened. I reacted. In and out, my knife sliced through his skin like butter. His hand relaxed, and I stepped back. Shock then anger darkened his blue eyes, and his lips pulled back in a sneer. "You bitch." His body tensed.

My guards closed in to take care of him. I made eye contact with them, expecting them to advance. They didn't. They looked over my right shoulder. Then I felt him behind me. The heat of his body and the familiar smell of sandalwood and coffee wrapped around me, soothing my agitated state of mind a bit but not enough to still my instincts. My security detail should have handled the threat in front of me, but they hadn't. That told me everything about who was at my back, even though my body didn't get the memo, and my reactions flared before I could stop them.

I lashed out, twisting my wrist and thrusting my hand backward. A vice clamped around my hand and stilled the momentum before the blade pierced skin. His arm extended over my opposite shoulder with a gun in hand—pointing at the center of the asshole's forehead. Blind panic swelled within me from the inability to move my arm, but then I heard the deep rumble of Stefano's voice, and the wave of fear paused, failing to crash over my head.

"Do you know who we are?" Menace dripped from Stefano's question, and I shivered.

Pedestrians gasped and surged away from us, creating a wide berth, and I was sure someone called the cops. It didn't matter, though, as they were on our payroll. We owned the city. The only one who would end up in handcuffs if they came was the guy standing in front of me with the stab wound to his upper arm.

The asshole's eyes widened, and he held up his hands, palms facing us. "I meant no disrespect."

"But you did disrespect her. So what's stopping me from putting a bullet in the center of your forehead?"

The tension in my shoulders eased, and a slow smile curved my lips. Vindication. That was what Stefano was giving me.

"I'm sorry." The man bowed his head. "Please forgive me. I thought you were someone else. It won't happen again."

"No." The feral growl in my voice indicated how precariously I toed the line of maintaining control. The urge to draw more of his blood was fierce, and I wanted to, but maybe it wasn't necessary. "It won't happen again because if you enter my sight, you'll die. There will be no second warning."

The asshole was shaking, his head bobbing in understanding as he inched a cautious step back. "I understand. I'm moving tonight. You won't see me again."

Stefano kept his gun trained on the guy as he quickened his pace then ducked into the shop next door to the deli. When only the two of us remained, he lowered his weapon, but his hand remained on mine that held the knife. "Let's go."

He drew me down the sidewalk and back to the coffee place. My guards followed. Once inside, we went to the back, and my security took positions at the front and rear entrances.

I was hyperaware of Stefano's body heat at my side and the blood that was congealing on the tip of my knife. He herded me into the back room where the employees took their breaks, released my hand, then locked the door.

I missed the heat of him. There were so many obstacles, and all I wanted was for Stefano to take me into his arms, effectively shutting out the world. If only his father wasn't such an issue, limiting the time his son had to fraternize with our family.

Frank must have had plans for his son, but whatever they were, they did not include me. When the tip had come in about where I was being held in Italy, Stefano was forbidden to assist. He hadn't listened and instead defied his father. Retribution for his disobedience had to have happened, but I didn't know what had gone down. All I knew was that I'd seen less of Stefano since I'd returned, and it broke my heart.

He was the one who made me feel safe. He was the one I'd been in love with for as long as I could remember. If only we had the freedom to be together… if I could have taken that next step toward a physical relationship with him, I would have. Having sex without a panic attack or the inability to enjoy it were things I worried about, as a vital part of me had died back in the hands of the traffickers, and I wasn't sure it would ever return. But my attraction to Stefano had not once waned. There was still hope.

A part of me was feral, birthed when I was taken, and fed by my abductors. I'd killed as many of them as I could. But even at my most vulnerable, they couldn't get to the core of what made me who I was—Mafia born, already bred from darkness. It wasn't an easy life, and we were all trained to overcome hellish situations. That ugly period in my life was no different. I survived and emerged stronger for it, an equal to Stefano in every way if you looked past my outer appearance to the monster that lurked within. I had loved him since we were young, and time only strengthened the bond we had yet to succumb to entirely.

I was capable of gentleness, humor, and love, but that went hand in hand with the ability to put a bullet in an enemy's forehead and not lose an ounce of sleep. My brother had tried to shield me the best that he could, as did my mother in the hours we'd spent together in the kitchen, but there was no escaping what was in our blood. We were royalty, and there was no denying our birthright.

"Emiliana."

His calm, deep voice snapped me out of my head and back to the storage room with him. He'd eased the knife from my tight grip and cleaned it. Then he pushed the sleeve of my sweater up and fitted the weapon back into the spring-loaded sheath strapped to my forearm. Pings of electricity trailed his fingers as he drew my sleeve back down my arm.

My reaction to him wasn't dead—far from it—and I wanted to explore it to see how far I could go without losing my mind. I hated his father for keeping us apart. Not only did I love Stefano, but he was my salvation.

CHAPTER THREE

STEFANO

I didn't like the blank look in Em's eyes as I took the knife from her hand, washed it, then returned it to where it belonged, strapped to her arm. Her face was pale, and she still hadn't responded to me as we stood in The Coffee Stop's employee break room. I shouldn't have been there, but I wanted a few moments to try to help her. Getting her off the sidewalk and away from people so she could catch her breath and deal with the trigger of a stranger grabbing her was how I planned to do that.

I clenched my jaw, frustrated that I let that asshole live. He'd scared her. That alone was enough for me to want to end him. The only reason I hadn't was because I wasn't sure whether putting a bullet in his forehead would send her into a full-blown spiral. We knew a lot about what had happened to her but not everything, or if there were more triggers. She didn't even know. Her mind had blocked a good portion of her experience, and I hoped for her sanity that she never remembered.

I said her name, and she blinked. Long, spiky lashes shadowed high cheekbones until she lifted them, revealing her gorgeous near-black eyes. A spark of awareness returned, and I cataloged everything about her as I waited for her to respond. A bloom of color spread across her features, and my gaze dropped to her full, pouty lips before jerking back to her almond-shaped eyes. Her dark hair framed her face and fell over her shoulders, down to her midback. It was soft and silky, and I longed to run my fingers through it, but touching her would have been selfish and not in her best interest unless she was fully present.

Her lips parted with a small puff of air. "I'm okay."

The sound of her voice and the way she looked at me like I was her anchor sent a volley of almost impossible-to-deny desire spiraling through me. Emiliana was a siren, my kryptonite. Having the strength to resist her, which I did to save her, easily brought me to my knees every damn time. But if I gave in, her safety would have been at great risk because Frank Rossi, my boss and father, would stop at nothing to destroy her and anyone who stood in his way. I was to have no one but to remain at his beck and call at all times, completely devoted and with no distractions or room for advancement. In essence, he owned me—*for now*. I had been born in darkness and sentenced to an eternity of it.

Em closed the distance between us, wrapped her arms around my waist, then rested her head on my chest.

At close to six foot three, I towered over her as I hugged her, reveling at how right she felt in my embrace. "What happened? Do you know who that was?"

"No." She snuggled closer, and I fought back a moan as her curves pressed against me. "I've never seen him before. Then when he grabbed me…"

The shrug told me what I already knew. He'd triggered something in her. She didn't like to be touched. Not anymore, and only by family and close friends. I was grateful to be included in that small inner circle.

Enzo would have a report about the guy soon, one he would share with me. My arms tightened around Em as a tremor ran through me. *What if I hadn't been there in time?* I didn't think I would survive anything happening to her, not again. The last time had almost destroyed me.

"Let's get you back." It was a risk to take her myself, but I didn't want to leave her unprotected. And I needed to know if that guy who'd grabbed her was an overzealous asshole or someone my dad had sent. Despite my words, I held her tightly, one hand at her lower back and the other cupping her head. I wasn't ready to let her go. I never was.

"I-I… oh God, Stefano. I messed up, didn't I?" She sniffed, and I closed my eyes for a brief second. "I'm so screwed up."

"No." I moved her back so that I could see her face, and she mine. "You're not. You're fierce and brave. No one has a right to lay their hands on you unless you permit them to." I wanted to kill that guy for upsetting her.

She shrugged, her teeth worrying her lower lip and drawing my attention. "Maybe it wasn't so bad to stab that guy. I did warn him, which is more than I used to do."

"I don't think you did enough. If I hadn't worried about it bothering you, I would have pulled the trigger."

A smirk curved her mouth. "Why would that bother me?"

I should have stepped back. I didn't. I traced her lower lip with my thumb, and she shivered. To resist Emiliana was torture, something I was well versed in but unwilling to experience in that moment. I bent my head, moving slowly so she had time to pull back. When she tilted her head to meet me, I brushed my lips across hers in a gentle caress. She trembled then wound her arms around my neck, giving me all the permission I needed.

My tongue traced the seam of her soft lips, begging entry. When she parted on a gasp, I slipped inside, teasing and tasting. The room fell away, and there was only her, the woman I'd been secretly in love with since we were kids. She was back in my arms, where she always should have been.

We'd kissed a few times before, long ago, and the memories haunted me. She was too beautiful, full of life, and unattainable. I would have tainted her very existence. So I'd done the right thing. I'd kept my distance until the next time she found me alone, and I broke, unable to resist the sheer temptation of the woman I'd coveted even though my father drilled into my head that he would take anything I wanted from me. I couldn't let him harm Emiliana. He could never know that I loved her. Nor could she.

It was wishful thinking. He'd found out I had feelings for her and used my "weakness" against me to ensure my compliance in whatever scheme he'd cooked up. But his time was limited. I had friends who'd risen the ranks to become their families' bosses: Enzo Vitale, Max Caruso, and Marco La Rosa. We were all around the same age, early- to midtwenties, with ancient souls dripping in blood and death. Together, we were devising a strategy that would put me in the position to take over my family, usurping my father's authority.

I shoved the pressing thoughts from my mind and enjoyed the feel of Emiliana and the sweetness of how she tasted against my tongue. Her fingers tangled in the hair at the back of my neck. When she angled her head to deepen the kiss, I knew I was in a world of trouble and slowed our pace until I drew back and broke away. I rested my forehead against hers, struggling for control. She would be the death of me. I craved her above all else, but to keep her safe, I had to resist for a while longer.

Her eyes were glazed over, her features soft and sexy. I wanted nothing more than to lose myself in her, but that wasn't the right way to make her mine. She deserved so much more, and I needed to set things up so that I could give it to her.

"Come here." I released her from the circle of my arms and took hold of her hand, leading her to the navy-blue couch against the wall. We sat, and I stretched my arm along the back. "Tell me how you're feeling." I toyed with her fingers. "I know what a stranger touching you did, and I need to understand where you're at right now." I worried I was making things worse with how I couldn't stop touching her.

She threaded our fingers together, stilling my movements. "I promise you, I'm fine."

Her smile transformed her face, and I fought myself from pushing her back onto the cushions and kissing her again. "I grew up with sisters. I know 'fine' is a dangerous word. Talk to me."

She rolled her eyes. "Stefano, stop. I'm all right. It was a momentary thing, but I was present enough to talk to him first, stay in control, and demand that he let me go. The rest was on him. He didn't listen." She leaned her shoulder against the back of the couch. "I'm not afraid. I won't have a relapse. What happened will not change anything, so you can stop worrying about me."

I never would, although keeping her in the dark wasn't smart, either, and there were things we had to discuss. "Has Enzo talked to you about the mole in the families?"

"Briefly." She sighed, clearly frustrated. "I wonder if the rat was in place when the guard abducted me four years ago."

"It's possible." I hated to admit it, but that made sense. Before we'd found out about the rat, we'd suspected something was wrong but could never find anything that proved it.

"I have no idea who it is. Sofia told me when she came back from Italy. So did Lil. We've been trying to figure it out too." She squeezed my hand. "I'm being smart. Don't worry about me." She pulled her hair back, and the diamonds I'd given her flashed in the light. "I don't leave home without these."

I grinned. "It's how I knew you were out of the house."

"I figured. Did you call Enzo? I would've expected him to come running too."

"Yeah, I let him know you were fine. We'll know who that guy was soon and whether there's cause for worry."

"If there is, we'll hunt him down. Together." Her gaze turned fierce. "Do not leave me out of this. It's my right."

There was no way in hell I would let her anywhere near a threat, and she knew it. Ignoring her demand, I changed the subject. "I have to keep my distance from you for a while longer. I don't want to, but—"

"Shh." She placed a finger over my mouth for the briefest of seconds. "I get it. Frank's dangerous and a major asshat."

I laughed because she wasn't wrong in her assessment. "If I'm cold or distant—"

"I'll know what you're doing. I wish things were different, but you can't hurt me with that, not after you kissed me the way you did. Do what you need to do. I'll be here when you're free."

I brushed my lips over hers once more before I drew her to her feet. I had to hand her over to her security detail outside the door to the employee break room, whether I wanted to or not. Frank could have spies anywhere, and the less we were seen together in public, the better. The plan to take power from my father burned even brighter inside me, as did the possibility of Emiliana being by my side once I took my rightful place in the family.

CHAPTER FOUR

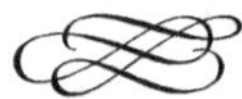

STEFANO

I slipped inside the warehouse where we held major meetings, information extractions, and sometimes executions for the Five Families. The moon was barely a sliver, which helped to minimize visibility. It was two in the morning, and I was meeting Enzo, Max, and Marco without anyone else privy to where I was. Enzo and I had been to hell and back to save his sister, Emiliana, with Max Caruso's aid. Max was Antonio's eldest and had met us in Italy to take down the entire trafficking ring. And Marco, oldest of the four La Rosa siblings, took the infiltration hardest. We'd lost one of our one, and I always wondered if he'd had feelings for Elena.

My cover, which I'd established with my friend Veronica several years before, was that I was in her arms. My father's spies told him that she was a woman I kept. Our arrangement was both beneficial and platonic—it looked as if we were lovers, but instead, it served to protect both of us.

My Mafia connections deterred her abusive ex. I paid her well so that she could provide for her child, and I gained the benefit of a cover story against my father and the ability to slip from her house undetected.

The dim light ahead illuminated Marco's tall frame as he hunched over the table, supported by his fists, his head bent and his dark hair falling forward to obscure his features. I understood the worry emanating from him. There was a lot we needed to uncover quickly before the wrong people were hurt.

As I neared, he straightened and pointed a gun at me, only lowering it when I moved from the shadows to provide a clear view of my face. Enzo and Max came in half a second later, and the sound of the bolt sliding home and locking us inside echoed through the large space.

We gathered around the table then took our seats. Strain etched around the other men's eyes and mouths, mirroring what I felt. But we were working together, something our fathers had failed to do, to solidify trust between the families that would enable us to unite and become stronger as allies. It was a mere technicality that Frank maintained his position. I would take it from him in a matter of time, and the other guys knew it.

"What did you learn about the asshole who grabbed Emiliana?" I asked Enzo. It drove me nuts that I hadn't heard a status update, even though the Vitale boss didn't answer to me—yet.

Enzo's square jaw hardened, his amber eyes darkening almost to his sister's near-black shade. "Not a damn thing. If there is a connection to Frank, we didn't see any indication of it or any other source that would raise a red flag."

"Did he leave town?" I needed to know he wasn't going to be a problem, or I would find him and ensure that he wasn't.

"Yeah." Enzo leaned back in his chair, tipping it onto two legs. "He threw several suitcases into an Audi and peeled out of there like we were already on his tail. I don't think he'll be a problem."

"We need to have more protection on your sister. That was too coincidental. I would bet everything I have on Frank making a move against her soon to prove a point to me."

"Have you done anything to piss him off?" Marco tapped the barrel of his gun on the table's surface.

I met his green-eyed gaze with a bored expression. "Nothing more than usual." He was on edge, and I wanted to know why.

"What have you learned? We all suspect Frank as the mole." Marco pointed the grip of his gun at me to make his point. "Have you spoken with your sister to find out if she knows anything?"

"Camila?" I raised my eyebrows. I hadn't talked to her since our father brokered her to the enemy. "There is no way to communicate with her without the Bratva hearing. I don't have spies within their organization, and if Frank does, I'm not privy to that information."

"I can't believe I'm saying this"—Enzo rubbed his hands over his face—"but Sofia has a connection with Katya."

Marco growled.

We'd seen her handiwork, the carnage she singlehandedly left in her wake.

"The Russian assassin is dangerous. Are you sure that's a good idea?"

"It is," Max interjected. "Katya would have access to all the members of the family. We don't know if Vic keeps Camila secluded or if he conducts business where she would be able to hear anything."

"True." I hated that I knew next to nothing about my sister and how she lived after being forced to marry the enemy. Vic stayed in the background. In the past, we'd dealt with Ivan or his father, Yuri, the most. "Katya might be our best bet, but I would like to talk to my sister without the Bratva listening in."

"I'll mention it to Sofia this morning," Enzo said. "We need to move faster to uncover Frank."

"If he's the rat. At this point, it's still speculation." Marco shifted to lean back in his chair. "I agree that it's a probable scenario. If we're wrong, we risk an unknown ambush."

I turned to Max. "What about Tony." Max's half brother had always been an untrustworthy pain in the ass.

"I have men watching him." Max shook his head then chuckled. "I didn't know what to do with the little shit, but he seems to be where he should be. Managing the club has driven the jealous little punk out of him."

Enzo smirked. "I can't see Tony as docile."

Max's lips twitched. "Hardly. But he's found his calling. From what you've all said and the reports I have on him from the past decade, he's a partier and happiest in the clubs. He took to the business side equally well."

"You don't trust him. Do you?" Marco sounded surprised. "We have to cover all angles. If Frank isn't the rat, Tony is next in line as a suspect."

"I wouldn't go that far," Max said. "He seems to have gained a new perspective since Antonio's death."

We weren't getting anywhere. "We won't disregard Tony, but our efforts need to focus on Frank." I glanced at the time on my watch. "I need to get back. Enzo, let us know when Sofia makes contact with Katya." After he nodded, I brought up what all of us were thinking. "The girls need protection. When one of us can't keep an eye on Em, Sofia, or Lil, then another of us must step up. Communication will be key in ensuring their safety."

I was terrified of something else happening to Emiliana, and knowing the guys had my back went a long way to free up my mind to lay the foundation for what we all agreed had to happen—forcing Frank to step down.

Emiliana

The sun crested the horizon as I cracked my neck, taking a few seconds to stretch. I looked around the dance studio that my brother had turned into a weapons-training room for me. The knives were fast and deadly. I could attack someone with a lethal throw from ten feet away before they had time to get their gun out of a holster. Not only that, but I'd learned the best places to hit to cause maximum damage. It wasn't anything new. Years of practice from when I was young instilled a rhythm, a symbiotic relationship, with the blades as an extension of my body.

When I was young, cooking with Mom was my main focus, along with spending time with my friends and family. But being born into the Mafia meant training since the time I could walk. I'd learned the deadliest strikes: brachial artery in the upper arm, carotid artery, heart, below the stomach from hip bone to hip bone, the femoral artery on the inside of the thigh, under the jaw, aiming toward the brain, and the abdominal aorta. Those vulnerable targets were drilled into me from child to adult until it was second nature. I needed to train and spar to survive. It gave me balance and reinforced that I was a weapon.

"The Sound of Silence" by Disturbed bled through the surround sound, which would soon morph into Evanescence as I moved the dummies and hanging bags of sand where I wanted them. I had to get out of my head. There were moments when the past was too close, the nightmare too real. It wouldn't leave me alone, but I would not let it win. No matter how much the wounds from Italy reopened, I refused to be a victim. I was stronger than that. They would not defeat me.

The knife dummies were in place, tennis balls hanging by strings, as were some of the sandbags. The others would drop randomly. I let the music's haunting and powerful melody seep into me as I twirled the spear-pointed blades. On the up beat, I launched forward with my arm raised, gliding through the air then arcing the blade in a downward swipe across the dummy's torso. To avoid the imaginary counterstrike, I dropped to my knees, sliding along the floor and arcing my body backward, my blade trailing behind me and catching the ankle. Foot planted, I pivoted and continued the cut across the Achilles tendons.

I created blurred faces on the dummies and sandbags. Through my mind's eye, I pictured my attackers and visualized their movements. I twisted, turned, and bent with each strike in a graceful dance around the targets. Adrenaline hummed through my body, fueling it as I flowed smoothly and efficiently with each cut and thrust.

A fine sheen of sweat coated my body for the third time through the minefield of pseudo attackers.

Once I eliminated the ghosts and satisfied my need to train, I took some time to regroup before I cleaned up the space in preparation for the next time I would be in here. Which wouldn't be long. I aimed for once a day, twice if the need arose. A small smile curved my mouth. I felt good. With the press of a button, I shut off the music, put my knives away, then let myself out of my studio to get ready. I was looking forward to Sofia and Lil coming over in a couple of hours.

***

Sofia burst through the front door with a wide grin I couldn't help but match. Lil wasn't far behind, and I laughed at the eye roll she gave to Sofia's exuberance. God, I'd missed my best friends. We didn't hang out nearly enough.

"What are we doing?" Lil dropped her purse on the hall table next to Sofia's.

I turned toward the kitchen. "Cooking, of course," I said over my shoulder. The ingredients were on the counter, and whether they liked it or not, it was what I wanted to do.

"Oh no." Sofia moved forward and touched my arm. "What happened?"

"Enzo didn't tell you?" I was genuinely confused. My brother worshipped the ground Sofia walked on and always had. I was under the impression that they didn't keep secrets from one another. Not any longer, especially after Italy.

"I was in the studio, working on my new clothing line for most of the day, but that was no excuse for him keeping whatever happened to himself." Sofia crossed her arms and impatiently tapped her foot.

Lil pulled out one of the island's stools, took a seat, and pursed her lips. Annoyance flashed in her light eyes. "Max didn't either." She nabbed a cookie that I'd baked earlier that morning. "Spill," she said through a bite.

I got a bottle of wine, opened it, poured each of us a glass, and told them everything that had happened with the asshole who grabbed me the day before. By the time I finished, Sofia had downed half of hers.

"Want to go after the guy?" Lil tapped her nails on the marble. "We have a pact to uphold. I say we find him and pay him a little visit tonight."

In our last year of college, after Marissa's violent murder in the dorms just before winter break, the three of us formed an agreement to band together against any obstacles we needed help with. Sofia and I would have done more with Benito, Lil's father, but she hadn't wanted us to get close to him, which had been hard. Sof and I wanted to defy her and get her the hell away from him. Thankfully, Max did what we couldn't.

And as much as I would've loved to enact some sort of revenge fantasy with them, it seemed like a moot point. "The guy fled. I think we're good." After glancing at the time, I grabbed the pot of boiling pasta and poured it out over the strainer. While it drained, I got the ingredients for the sauce going.

"I thought we were supposed to help?" Sofia poured more wine, topping off Lil's and mine while she was at it.

Lil chucked a piece of cookie at her, bouncing it off Sofia's head. "When do we cook? She says that but then does it all. We're here for support and to drink wine with her, like always."

I grinned. She wasn't wrong. "You both would screw it up anyway."

"Meh, I'm fine with that." Sofia picked up the piece of chocolate cookie that'd landed on the island and popped it in her mouth. "Did you know the guys met at the warehouse last night?"

"What?" That was news to me. "Why? And who, just the bosses?"

"Not quite," Lil said. "Max, Enzo, Marco, and Stefano."

"Huh. Enzo didn't say anything. Of course, he doesn't live here anymore." I looked pointedly at Sofia.

She rolled her eyes. "Like you want to live with Enzo forever. That would be like me wanting to have Trey, Nico, and Marco move it. I'm happy to be done with their slobby ways." Her look turned sly. "I'm surprised Stefano didn't tell you."

Heat crawled up my neck and settled in my cheeks. "Why would Stefano come over? He never does."

"When are you going to change things between you? Tell him how you feel?" Lil's voice softened. "He won't make a move until you tell him you want it."

"That's true," Sofia chimed in. "You were caught up in recovering, as you should've been, and couldn't have seen what he went through after bringing you back. I'd never seen anyone look more helpless and murderous at the same time before. I think, given the opportunity, he would move mountains for a chance to be by your side."

I thought over what they said, contemplating sharing what had happened between Stefano and me while combining the prosciutto with the sauce then tossing the rigatoni in. Once everything was mixed, I served the pasta onto plates then got the salad I'd made earlier out of the fridge.

Once settled at the island with them, I swirled my wine around, creating legs around the sides of the glass. "We'll have our time. It's just not now. There's too much unrest with finding the mole."

"Why do you have to wait? He has a place downtown. You could go on a date or to one of the clubs your family or Max owns," Lil offered.

Sofia moaned over a mouthful of pasta, and I smiled. I loved cooking. It centered me. We tried to share a meal at least once a week unless all hell broke loose, which wasn't unusual.

"I'm sure we will." I let them see the conviction in my eyes, because I would make sure that Stefano knew he was mine when the time was right. "After we learn who the rat is."

Sofia's hand covered mine. "It's your turn to find your happy, just like we did." She winked, and a dreamy haze glazed her eyes. "Before Enzo left for the meeting, he made sure—"

"No! Gross, Sofia." I yanked my hand from under hers and waved it around. "I don't want to hear anything about what you did with my brother in bed. Ick."

Lil laughed and shoved Sofia's shoulder. "That was mean. Speaking of awkward situations—thanks for that, Sof—do any of you know what's going on with Eva and Tony?"

"Aside from the fact that your cousin has a crush on your brother-in-law?" I couldn't help but cringe at the mental picture. Even though Tony was Max's half brother, I thought the title of brother-in-law still fit.

Sofia shuddered. "I can't figure out why she has a thing for Tony. I mean, he's a jerk, and I don't know. I still feel like he had something to do with Marissa's death. Not directly, because we know Ivan killed her, but… did they fight beforehand? Did Tony hit her?"

"It's weird and hard to let go of the mistrust we have for

him." I'd never liked Tony. And when we thought he was the one who'd killed our friend, that had only escalated. "Marissa, Eva, and Tony used to party together. A lot. I would think that Eva would be suspicious too."

"But she never was. She's always loved Tony, and he's used her, exploiting the emotional commitment she has to him." Lil helped herself to the salad, putting it in a bowl. "I know the guys think that Frank is the rat, but what if they're wrong? What if it was Tony all along?" We exchanged horrified glances as silence stretched between us.

"I think it's time we look into what he's doing ourselves." Sofia met our gazes with determination. "The guys are busy checking into and watching Frank. Let's take up the slack and do the same with Tony. Are you guys in?"

Lil and I agreed, and I braced myself for what was to come. I would have to go into clubs where there were many people and no Stefano to have my back. But it was worth it. The sooner we flushed out the rat, the sooner he and I would have a chance at a real relationship instead of a few stolen moments in the shadows.

At the thought of the rare encounters we'd shared, one memory surfaced of being at his home and hanging out with his sister, Marissa, and our other friends.

My hand had trailed along the wall, the bracelet Marissa let me borrow jingling as I moved. It was dark in that part of the house. Forlorn. Heavy. The place made me deeply uncomfortable, as if the walls wept for the suffering it witnessed.

But Stefano had passed by Marissa's room, where we were sorting through her jewelry on the bed, and I wanted to say hi to him, no matter how creepy the place was. He never hung out with us. Besides, he'd paused for a moment when his gaze landed on me. I didn't imagine the heat in it or how he ignored everyone else in the room.

"I didn't realize your brother was going to be home. Neither did Enzo." I held still while Marissa bent over my wrist, fastening another bracelet to it.

She shrugged. "I guess."

I shared a glance with Sofia. It was always a little strange in Marissa's house. Her dad wasn't supposed to be home that day, so her mom said we could come over. It wasn't often that we did, and my mom didn't like me there. Usually, she sent my brother with me.

Sofia flopped back on the bed. "You're boy crazy."

I scowled at her. "Really? And how are you when my brother is around?" I made a fake gagging sound because she attached to Enzo at the hip whenever she got the chance. He didn't mind, but I sometimes did. I stole a peek at Marissa from under my lashes as she straightened. *Does Marissa feel that way about me too?*

She laughed, her cheeks turning pink. "True, but Enzo and I are friends. Stefano usually ignores us."

Not me. He definitely paid attention to me if his father wasn't around. And it was one of those times—I wanted to take advantage of it. I missed the way his lips felt on mine.

I slid off the bed, and Lil scooted over, riffling through the pile of trinkets we were looking at. The longer it was since he'd walked past the door, the more anxious I got. I needed to see him, if only for a few seconds. "I was supposed to tell him something from Enzo. I'll be right back."

Sofia grinned, and heat crawled up my neck to settle in my cheeks. She knew what I was doing. Marissa mumbled as she pulled a ring from the pile, which she followed with an exclamation over finding what she was looking for.

"Hurry back. We need to figure out what we're doing about the party tonight."

I nodded to Marissa. I didn't want to go. We were in our last year of middle school, and the party she was talking about was a high school one. If our brothers were there, we could go. No one would mess with us because it meant their death. People knew what we were. It was just that the party scene wasn't my thing. Stefano, on the other hand, was.

He was two years older than me, a sophomore in high school and already towering over me at six feet tall, the same height as his father, and no sign that he was done growing.

My heart pounded as I sped through the hallways in search of him. The next corner would lead me to the stairs toward the back of the house. I turned the corner, and an arm snaked around my waist. I let out a shriek as a steel band wrapped around my stomach then pulled me into a dark room. With my back pressed against the wall, my heart beat against my sternum, but not in fear. I recognized his touch and the feeling of his lips as they moved urgently over mine.

I slid my hands up his chest and over his broad shoulders then looped my arms around his neck. His hand buried in my hair, cupping my head. My lips parted under his insistence, and I moaned as his tongue teased mine. Surrounded by Stefano's strong embrace, I felt wanted, cherished.

My head spun, the room we were in fading away as he stoked the fire in my core to unbearable heights. I wanted him, consequences be damned. When his hand slid beneath my shirt, I shivered at the first touch against my skin. His large palm spanned my back then slid around to cup my breast. My head fell back as I gasped. His lips left mine to trail down my neck, and his thumb moved back and forth over my nipple as I strained for more.

Then he was off of me, and I stumbled forward. He caught me, but with one look at his stricken face, I knew our time had come to a swift halt. The deep rumble farther down the hall told me why. His father was home. Stefano stayed far away from me if the man was around. My heart raced for an entirely different reason as we stood, frozen to the spot, hoping Frank Rossi wouldn't walk down the hallway but would remain downstairs.

Either way, I had to get the hell out of there. It was never good to be caught unaware and alone with that man.

I shook myself free from the past, wishing with my whole heart that someday the obstacles that kept us apart would topple and we could be together.

CHAPTER FIVE

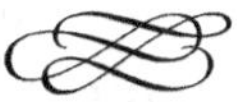

EMILIANA

Lil and Sofia had stayed late, and we'd talked for hours, watched movies, and eaten dinner together. I felt immensely better after spending the day with them. Even the brush with the jerk who'd grabbed me failed to bother me anymore. I'd handled that with more clarity than I'd had in years. For the first time in a long while, I could say with confidence that I was doing well. My trigger was still there but no longer overwhelming. If that guy had touched me even months before, I would have gutted him. But I almost stayed fully present and in the moment, and I was proud of that.

With a glance out the window at the partially cloudy day, I was glad I'd put on my favorite oatmeal-colored cable-knit cardigan. I'd just taken a sip of coffee when my phone pinged with an incoming text from Eva: *Go shopping with me.*

Me: *What? Why me? Did you ask Sof?*

Sofia was the shopping queen, and Eva usually preferred going with her.

Eva: *Sof is out w/ Enzo buying furniture or some lame shit like that.*

I sent a quick text to Lil because I was not a huge shopper, and Eva was exhausting. The only one who didn't mind her was Sofia because she, too, had boundless energy when it came to anything retail-related.

Lil: *Can't. Sorry! At an art museum w/ Nicole.*

What is going on today? And I would not have pegged Nicole as one to enjoy an art museum. Then again, she had changed a lot since becoming a widow. Having Lil as a daughter-in-law had brought a sense of purpose back into her life. She'd cut down on the drinking and stopped visiting the plastic surgeon. I guessed it made a weird kind of sense—even though Lil didn't advertise it, she was an artist, and Nicole might have taken an interest to show support for what was important to her new daughter-in-law.

I texted Eva, saying I would join her, and made arrangements to meet her at my favorite boutique on Michigan Avenue. There was enough time to finish my coffee and toast and change, but then I would have to be on my way. I messaged Enzo with my plans. Rather than worry Stefano, I left my diamond teardrop earrings at home. I gave the guard a heads-up next. It was crazy that I had to let my family know anytime I went out, but they worried, and it wasn't asking too much. I liked knowing that they were apprised of my whereabouts, at least until things were a little safer for the family.

It didn't take long to finish getting ready and make sure I had an arsenal of weaponry on me and the security detail in place before heading out. The drive into the city was nice. A couple of the guards had left as soon as I'd given them the itinerary for today and went to secure parking for when I arrived. They knew the stores we would go to and had checked out the first two, making sure they were safe. There would be a guard positioned at the front and rear entrances before I got there.

The sidewalks were busy as I got out of the car. I wove through the congestion then went into the boutique and scanned the store for Eva. She wasn't anywhere in sight. My phone pinged a few minutes later with a text message from her. She was running behind. Eva was perpetually late. I should have expected nothing less.

I smiled at the thirtysomething honey-blond manager. "Morning, Celia."

"Good morning, Ms. Vitale. How can we help you today?"

I pursed my lips, looking around the high-end store. "I'm looking for more day wear, with a few evening items thrown in." I was such a sucker for fall clothing. I spotted a formfitting knit dress in a burnt red that would look amazing with my hair and skin tone. I found my size, trailing my fingers over the buttery-soft material. I loved the softness of the clothes they carried most—luxury in the best ways.

"I'll have Presley get a dressing room started for you. Would you like anything to drink? A latte or champagne?"

I grinned. It was ten in the morning, and I had no desire for champagne. "I'm fine, thank you." I picked out a few more things while Presley gathered armfuls under Celia's instruction and took them to the dressing room in the back. They would shut it down for me, not allowing anyone else back there. "Eva will be here soon."

Celia's eyes sparkled a little brighter. "We had a delivery this morning. Some of the girls are unpacking it now. I'll have them bring a selection to the sales floor immediately."

I had to laugh because I understood. Sofia and Eva's shopping expeditions were legendary. I could practically hear a cheery *cha-ching* from the credit card machine on the sales desk. Apparently, Celia could too.

I plucked a silky blue-gray long-sleeved T-shirt in the softest material I thought I'd ever felt off the rack to take back with me. There was no use waiting for Eva. She would be a whirlwind when she arrived, trying on clothing and making decisions twice as fast as I did. She did not mess around on a shopping mission.

Classical music played quietly throughout the store as I took a few more choices with me to try on. It was probably better that I'd gotten there before Eva, so I wasn't rushed or having to show her everything. While I didn't mind doing that with Lil and Sofia, it irritated me a little with Eva. We had very different tastes, and she didn't always understand that. Still, she was fun to be around, and I was looking forward to her liveliness.

"Do you need anything else?" Celia glided into the softly lit changing area, which had been designed like a bridal shop.

"No. Just send Eva back when she gets here." I grinned at Celia, knowing she'd prepped the sales staff for the Tasmanian devil that was coming.

"Press the call button if you need different sizes or anything at all, Ms. Vitale. It's always a pleasure to have you here."

I nodded then browsed through what Presley had selected for me. There were many promising outfits, and I was suddenly glad I'd agreed to shop with Eva. The dressing room was large and spacious, and the lack of other shoppers was fantastic. Being in the Mafia had its perks.

The long-sleeved tee was first, and I exchanged my sweater for it. The jeans I had on looked great with the shirt, and I smoothed my hand over my stomach. It would be a favorite. I needed to see if it came in any other colors. I would have loved a dark-red one too.

The thin material outlined the knives strapped to my forearms, and I grinned. I couldn't wear it with those. I would have to be creative with the weapons I armed myself with when I had it on. I could always use the steel hairpins, and I had several of them. They were gorgeous, and I added them whenever I had an excuse to.

There was a soft scuff, and I whirled around. I scanned the room as I inched from the area where I was changing.

A dark form with a ski mask obscuring his face came out of nowhere, leading a pack of three.

I kicked out, knocking the gun from the first offender's hand. It clattered to the floor, the sound echoing in the dressing room.

The doors to the dressing room burst open, and my guards spilled in. I let them handle the two others but called them off when they advanced on the guy I was fighting. He was mine.

As I slid my knife free of the sheath strapped to my wrist, I let the darkness that lived inside of me unfurl. I wanted to spill his blood. I craved it. Something dangerous had been birthed a little over four years before, and I was more than ready to let it out to play.

I danced with the enemy, parrying and thrusting. Neither of us had drawn first blood—yet. He twisted, an arm extended. As I jerked to the side, his leg shot out, slamming into my stomach. The air whooshed out of me, and I flew back into the wall. He advanced. My hand tightened on the handle of my blade. I dropped to my knees as his fist slammed into the wall where my head would have been. Arm extended, I sliced up from the inside of his groin, going for the femoral artery.

His fingers latched onto my hair, and he yanked hard. Jolts of pain exploded over my scalp. The intent was clear in his dark eyes, and I readied for the blow that was coming.

I lifted my left arm to intercept. My forearm slammed into his wrist, stopping the downward arc of his knife hand aimed for my neck. I sensed my guards closing in. They weren't going to let me have it, but I needed it. There wasn't any more time before they took him down. I had to end him.

He shoved me back, and I let him, using the momentum to twist and swing my hand, still clutching the knife, to slice his forearm. A stutter step had me facing him once more, but I couldn't stop from flying backward. As I slammed into the wall, he followed. The tip of his blade pierced my shoulder. My right arm came up in defense, the blade poised and ready. I buried it into his forearm. He lost small-motor mobility and dropped his knife. His momentary shock gave me enough time to go for the gun I had tucked into the waistband of my jeans.

With murder in his eyes, he yanked the knife from his arm. I shot him twice in the chest and once in the forehead. The guards pulled his dead weight away so he wouldn't fall on me.

Ren, the captain of my security detail, bent in a crouch in front of me. "Are you hurt?" His gaze crawled over me, cataloging the blood that wasn't mine, then returned to my shoulder. His finger hooked on the fabric of the ruined shirt, and he tore it wider, exposing the insignificant cut.

I brushed his hands away. "I'm fine. It's only a scratch."

The tension around Ren's jawline told me he wasn't happy with my order to keep them at bay while I'd fought. But he understood why I'd needed to do it. The darkness that lived in me was something he'd helped me hone into a weapon while training. That was why he'd listened to my calling them off, at least for a while.

He leaned back on his heels, giving me a little space, just as Eva rushed inside, her gun drawn. When she saw the bodies on the ground, she dropped her gun. It clattered to the floor as she raced to my side with wide eyes. "What the hell happened? Are you okay?" She took my hand in hers and squeezed the life out of it.

I extricated my crushed fingers then gently patted the top her hers. "I'm fine. Promise."

The guys were pulling off the ski masks to reveal who'd ambushed me when Eva sucked in a breath.

"What is it?" I sat up straighter, craning my neck to see around Ren's large form. Eva had a different angle. I wasn't sure which of the attackers had alarmed her. "Do you know who they are?"

She caught her lower lip between her teeth for a second before answering. "I don't know them, but I've seen them on Tony's security team."

I pushed to my feet to get a better view as Ren snapped pictures of their faces and sent them to Enzo. Eva was freaking the hell out. I needed to get her out of there. "Hey"—I went over to my yes pile then thrust the clothes into her arms—"can you take these to Celia and have her ring them for up for me?" I glanced at the ruined shirt I was wearing. I pinched the hem of the tee. "Tell her about this. I'll buy it, but I want another in the same size, and ask if she has a red one. I want that too."

"Oh, sure." Distracted by the clothes and the task, she pivoted to go into the storefront.

I could hear her exclaiming over a sweater dress. She would have her own pile, probably twice the size of mine, purchased before I was ready to go.

I shifted my attention back to Ren. He ordered one of his men to get going on cleanup. My soldiers hefted the dead bodies over their shoulders. Another guard must have pulled a car up to the back door because they were going out that way to put them in the trunk. There was blood on the carpet and splattered on one portion of the wall. Someone made a call then announced that a cleaning service would be there within half an hour.

Someone handed me a first aid kit, and I got to work, disinfecting the scratch with alcohol wipes. Once I'd secured butterfly strips and gauze, I changed back into my sweater. Just in time, too, as my brother barged into the back room with Sofia on his heels.

I was so glad that I was dressed and had the small injury covered. "I'm fine. Promise." I held my hands up to my brother, palms out.

Sofia pursed her lips, looking at the bloodstains then back at me. She raised her eyebrows, and I grinned in response, to which she shook her head then came to stand by me as Enzo growled at my security guards. Then she linked our arms and shouted over her shoulder at my brother that we weren't needed so we were going to shop as she drew me toward the front of the store.

As soon as we were clear, she leaned toward me conspiratorially. "You know he's going to call Stefano, right?"

My head knocked back, and my mouth formed an O. *That can't be good.*

CHAPTER SIX

STEFANO

Adrenaline pumped through my body as I paced, the need to go to Emiliana almost impossible to deny. Too many times, I'd failed in protecting my sisters and my mother, and I would be damned if anything would happen to Em. I ground the heels of my hands against my closed eyelids, trying to keep the past at bay. It didn't matter. My sister Marissa's voice was circling in my head, taunting me with all I'd lost.

And just like that, the years faded, and I was back in the house I'd grown up in with my family. The soft knock on my bedroom door told me it was one of my sisters. I pushed off the floor, ignoring the way my back ached from the healing bruises. The room was dark when I opened the door to find Marissa standing on the opposite side of it, wringing her hands. Alarm shot through me. "What's wrong?"

"Nothing." She grabbed the end of her braid and twisted it. "Are you okay? I heard Dad..."

"I'm fine." I didn't want to talk about it. The beating was one of many, just another day in my fucked-up life with a monster for a father and a weak mother who did nothing to stop him. Someday, I would grow big and tall, and if I kept working out with Marco and his brothers, I would have muscles. Only then would it stop.

For the time being, I did everything I could to listen to his conversations and learn about his business dealings. I knew one day, the things I uncovered would work in my favor.

"Oh, okay." Marissa's words were soft. "Can I come in for a minute?"

"Dad isn't back yet, right?" It was safer for her if she stayed away from me if he was home. He had already used veiled threats toward my sisters against me, and lately, he'd said he could make the others disappear if need be. He never named who, but I knew he was talking about Marissa's friends. It was a threat I wouldn't take lightly.

"No. Mom said he would be gone all day."

I opened the door wide and stepped back. Marissa entered on silent feet. Another thing we'd learned well—never be heard. A mistake could cost us so much. Maybe it would have cost my sisters less than it did me, but they were still terrified of him.

Mom protected her daughters by keeping them close as much as possible. To my father, that was where my sisters belonged until he had another use for them. The day he deemed them ready, he would marry them off for the price that fit his needs. We never knew what or when. There was time, though, as we were all too young to be of much use to him. I was being groomed to take over the business. But I wasn't a fool. He would never relinquish control. Still, I had to learn whatever he deemed necessary to work under him, which was where he planned on keeping me.

One day, I would take everything from him. I lived for that day.

Marissa hopped up on my bed, and I sat with her, resting my back against the headboard. With only two years between us, she came to me rather than our sister, who was the oldest.

Marissa was like a ray of light, and I adored her. Her personality was so different than mine. I was analytical, calculating, and goal-oriented. She was carefree, wild, and artistic, unless our father was around. Then she was silent and tried her best to blend in like the rest of us.

I studied her heart-shaped face and how her lips were pressed tight. "What's wrong? What aren't you telling me?"

She shrugged her thin shoulders. "Mom said my friends could come over, but I'm worried about Emiliana. She doesn't always stay in the room. What if Dad comes home and finds her?"

Emiliana and Sofia had parents who weren't cruel like Lil's and ours. Marissa and I worried that our friends couldn't see past the mask our father wore and ventured into dangerous territory. We both watched out for them.

Our father didn't like it when Marissa had people over. Camila wasn't as outgoing, so it hadn't been a problem with our older sister. If he came home and was angry about a work meeting he'd had, we just weren't sure what would happen. "I'll watch out for her."

She grabbed my hand and squeezed. "Thanks, Stefano."

I would do anything for my sisters and Emiliana. I didn't understand it, but I was drawn to her, and I couldn't let my father hurt her. Part of me thought that my younger sister knew how I felt about Em because I had a hard time staying away when her friend was over, even though it was best that I did.

With a roar, I shoved the memory back where it belonged— in the past. Another check at the time and my teeth ground together.

It had been hours since Enzo texted the photos and disclosed what had happened to Emiliana. I wanted to see her, but it wasn't a good idea. Something was going on with my father. That evil glint in his eye was even more prevalent, and he'd shut himself in his office for a phone call. He'd been behaving even more oddly than usual, and that was enough cause for concern.

In the kitchen, I grabbed a sandwich the cook had left in the fridge for me and dialed the number of our arms liaison. There was a shipment of weapons arriving, and I had to check the progress. They were due to unload into the basement of one of our warehouses on the south side. After confirming a few details, I hung up then polished off the rest of the food, contemplating our other big moneymaker—medical insurance fraud.

The arms deals often went off without a hitch, so I monitored the insurance fraud closely. We had several companies set up, and my job was to check in with the managers each day, doing a sweep of the entries made on the previous one. It was big money, and we funneled some of it through a club and hotel that we'd opened last year.

After finishing the immediate tasks, I made my way through the house to my father's office. I could hear the low murmur of his voice through the thick door but not the actual words. I rapped my knuckles on it, waiting for him to give the okay to enter. A few seconds passed before he bellowed "come in."

I opened the door then did a quick visual sweep of the room to make sure he was alone. With the blinds tightly closed, no moonlight entered the space.

My father prepped a cigar then lit it. After a couple of puffs, he motioned for me to sit opposite him, something I didn't want to do but did anyway. I briefed him on business then waited to see if he would divulge whatever scheme he had brewing, which I wasn't entirely sure I wanted to hear. But I needed information about his clandestine dealings. If he was indeed the rat—and I was almost positive he was—I needed proof.

He leaned back in his chair, his lips curving into that self-righteous expression I hated as the hand holding his cigar hovered close. "I've gotten word that Elena Caruso is alive."

I held still. That was news I hadn't expected. "Is she in Italy?

The trafficking ring was dismantled over four years ago." When Enzo and I went in search of Emiliana, we'd heard of Elena's disappearance. We'd even found her clothes and DNA. Given where the stab wounds had been on her shirt and the blood, we determined that she hadn't survived. If she had and we'd left her there… my fists clenched beneath his desk. At a young age, I'd learned never to let him see how his words or actions affected me.

"We don't know where she is." He puffed a few more times, his observant, beady eyes trained on me.

"Why are we involved? She's a Caruso. Tony and Max would be the ones to locate and bring her back."

"They aren't going to know we have her. Now"—he leaned farther back in his leather chair—"you're on good enough terms with the new Vitale boss. I expect you to find out what he knows and report back to me."

"I hardly see how this is vital to our organization. Have someone else do it." I needed more information about why he was interested in her. But I had a sinking suspicion that he planned to open a prostitution or trafficking ring—something I would never allow. Frank Rossi's reign of terror had to come to an end.

There was a knock at his door. When my father said to enter, I turned in my seat so that my back wasn't completely exposed and I could see who it was. Drago, my father's advisor, entered—the raised and roughened scar from his cheek to chin could have identified him from a mile away. I nodded a greeting, hiding the mixed feelings I had about him. He'd screwed me over too many times, his loyalty to my father appearing solid. I wasn't entirely sure, though. His behavior had seemed more like a survival mechanism a couple of times when I'd caught a slight wince at one of Frank's orders against my sisters or mother.

"Let's try this again," my father boomed, and I jerked my

gaze back to him. "Get the information about Elena's whereabouts and deliver it to me."

I hesitated too long. The small prick at my neck was an indication of that, and my vision wavered. The drug Drago gave me moved through my system quickly. My last thought before I succumbed to the drug was that for Emiliana's safety, I would have to agree to find Elena's location.

My head pounded in a vicious beat, and my arms, wrists, and shoulders screamed from being tethered to a beam overhead. I didn't need my vision to clear to know where I was or what condition I was in. It wasn't the first time my father had strung me up by the rafters in the basement. It was his torture chamber, where he liked to take anyone who dared to defy him even in the slightest way, including all of the members of his family at one point or another.

We'd learned at a young age to agree with whatever he asked, no matter how wrong it was. I was the only one who had defied him more times than were healthy. It was a miracle I was still breathing.

I cleared my mind of everything, including the worry over Emiliana. He hadn't threatened her. But she was close by, and it would be too easy for him to grab her and hurt her, especially since he knew she meant something to me. Me defying his orders and joining Enzo to rescue her had pushed him over the edge. I'd paid the price when I'd returned by becoming a resident of the basement for a good portion of a week. He'd left me alive, but barely.

My current infraction against him had been minimal, and I could only hope my little session would be as well. I took inventory of everything I could. My shirt was gone but not my pants. There were no other sounds in the room, but the telltale smell of cigar smoke was heavy, which meant my father was nearby. There was no use in prolonging the inevitable.

My shoes were gone, but he hadn't ordered my ankles to be tied. I could get out by wrapping my legs around whoever's neck came the closest. A sense of resolve settled over me. That wouldn't help. I needed information, and my father liked to talk when we were down there. I'd learn more than I would in his office.

He would issue a threat to get me to do what he wanted. He always did. He didn't value anyone's life but his own. For years, he'd used Emiliana against me, and I'd done everything in my power to keep my emotions hidden where she was concerned. It was difficult because the handful of explosive kisses we'd shared were vivid in my memory, causing a tsunami of longing for what I could never have while my father drew breath.

The drug's effect hadn't fully dissipated, and I couldn't maintain my hold on the images I normally kept locked away and only took out when I was far from Frank's observant presence. But the feeling of her softness in my hands, the way she would gasp at the initial contact of our lips then the hungry way she'd respond were never far from my mind. I maintained a tight rein on my emotions, except where Emiliana was concerned. She alone could break through the wall.

The times I'd kissed her in a dark hallway, grabbing her before she could utter a sound, had been few and far between because doing so was a liability. I never wanted to make her the sacrificial lamb led to my father's slaughter. But those fleeting moments when I'd broken and pulled her heavenly body against mine, devouring her lips and reveling in the way she melted against me and responded with enthusiasm, provided a lifeline that kept me going through the hell of my existence.

I dreamed of a time when we could be together without the fear of my father harming her to get to me. It was getting harder to stay away from her, and I couldn't help but wonder if it was worse that I stayed away or if she would be safer if I were by her side, able to deflect any attack my father ordered against her.

As the last remnants of the drug faded, the dizziness and my vision cleared, but not the taste of death in my mouth. That would remain until I was released from this hellhole. Sadly, I could not fight my way out because I needed information, and it wasn't good to show all my cards—I'd never shown my father my true strength or fighting ability. The plan was to endure and hopefully gain something from my time down there.

I firmed my legs so that my toes bore some of the weight away from my wrists. The cement floor beneath me was cold, rough, and unforgiving. I knew without having to look that there was a drain not far behind me. The scent of blood and sweat had been washed away from whomever he'd had down there last. There was always someone. Frank Rossi was a sadistic bastard who ran the business with an iron fist. But even he made mistakes, and I would find and expose them. He wouldn't know what hit him when I struck.

"Good." My father's smoke-ravaged voice boomed from behind me. "You're awake."

His voice shifted as he circled where I hung, and I heard the unfurling of the whip in his hand. It looked like he would do the dirty work himself rather than ordering Drago to do it so that he wouldn't break a sweat. It must have been a special occasion. He'd gotten complacent with administering torture over the last few years.

The crack of the whip resonated in the room as he struck the cement floor. I braced myself because I knew his patterns. He would do that then hit me when he thought I wasn't expecting it. If I didn't respond the way he wanted, his fury would escalate as he unleashed his wrath on my body until he tired or I passed out.

At the first strike from the leather whip, I gritted my teeth. He hadn't hit me as hard as usual. My skin remained intact for the time being. It wouldn't last. He liked to watch me bleed. I blocked the pain, dulling myself to the consecutive strikes against my back.

"Why do you care so much about the Caruso girl?" I needed to know. Then I would go to Max so we could plan a counterattack.

"I don't answer to you!" he shouted. "Who's the boss of this family?"

Sadistic fuck. "You are." *But not for much longer.*

"Having you get the information from Enzo is a kindness. There are other methods I could employ instead."

I wanted to respond, but that would have been feeding the monster. We continued with the same pattern. I'd ask a question, hoping to gain insight. He'd roar then rail against my defiance, neither of us revealing anything. It was unusual, but it told me he wasn't acting alone. Ordinarily, he would brag about portions of his plan and how brilliant it was. He had to have been reporting to the Russians. Nothing else made sense. So I ceased with the inquisition and endured.

It wasn't until blood colored the floor that he spoke again, sealing my fate with his words. "Learn where Elena is from Enzo Vitale, or I'll drag your sister, Camila, back from Russia by her hair, and her death will be on your hands."

CHAPTER SEVEN

STEFANO

My back burned, and stabbing pain flooded my nerve endings every time I moved. I'd cleaned and bandaged my wounds as best I could. Then I'd gone to see Veronica, the woman who pretended to be my lover but was a front for an easy escape to hide where I went next.

It was around eleven at night, and she applied antibiotic cream and redid my bandages so that I wasn't leaking blood all over the place. It could have been worse. He could have poured salt in the wounds. I considered myself lucky that time. I hadn't passed out from what he'd done, and my back wasn't as bad as it could have been. I would heal. I dismissed the discomfort as best as I could.

The lights were off, as if we'd gone to bed. I waited twenty minutes before going out through the hidden door in her closet that led to an underground tunnel to the neighbor's shed. They never used it.

I'd had the escape path built years before. It would come in handy if Veronica ever needed to use it to escape her violent ex. Her kid's bedroom had a secret access door behind the bookcase that went directly to her mom's room, also behind a piece of furniture. They were designed to open with ease by depressing buttons beneath a book on the third shelf, second from the end. The added insurance and money that I gave her went a long way in securing her lifelong loyalty. Plus, she hated my father too. It was beneficial for both of us.

Once out of the neighbor's shed, I went to the apartment lot half a block away and got into the used car I kept there for such purposes, which I'd registered under a fake name. I drove the thirty minutes to Max's place, parked one neighborhood over, then made my way in on foot.

The blinds were drawn. The door in the back creaked open, and a slice of light split the night. I used my burner phone to let Max know I was there. I slipped through the door and followed Max in. Enzo lifted a whiskey in greeting. I dropped onto an armchair and accepted the drink Enzo poured for me.

"What's going on?" Max rested his elbows on his knees as he leaned forward.

I recanted my conversation with my father, minus the torture session, then reiterated that it appeared he was working with someone. Neither man was surprised.

"You knew Elena was alive?"

"It was why Ivan was after Sofia," Enzo said through clenched teeth. "He wanted her to tell him where Elena was."

I couldn't believe what I was hearing. "Why am I just now learning about this? Max?" I shifted to include him in my glare.

"I found out through Enzo." Max pushed out a weary breath. "That's all we know right now, that she's alive and not in the hands of the traffickers. Not where she is."

"Back to Frank," Enzo prodded.

"I think he's working with the Russians," I admitted. "That's what makes sense."

Max nodded. "It does. Frank and Antonio had connections with the Russians that we don't fully know about."

"This is the first I've heard about Elena, though. I don't know

why my father or the Russians are after her. And if she's alive"—
I ran my hand over my face, horrified at what she'd suffered all
those years—"we made a horrible mistake by not investigating
further." Enzo and Max shared a glance, and I narrowed my
eyes. "What else aren't you telling me?"

Enzo downed his whiskey before leveling his gaze at me.
Something dark swirled in his eyes. "Frank is working with the
Russians if he's looking for Elena."

"What we need to do is devise a false trail for Stefano to take
back to Frank," Max said. "I don't know why they want my
adopted sister so badly, and that's something we need to find
out." He looked at Enzo. "Ask Sofia. She's got an in with Katya."

"I don't want her dealing with the Russian assassin any more
than necessary. We should wait on that."

"Why?" I didn't see the problem. "She was already going to
find out if Katya had a way for me to talk to Camila."

"Fucking hell, I forgot about that." Enzo dropped his head
back and groaned. "I hate having her involved with Katya. She's
dangerous."

"She's been on Sofia's side all along. I wouldn't worry too
much," Max reasoned.

"Easy for you to say. Lil's demons are dead," Enzo shot back.

He had Max there. Benito had been her biggest problem.
Things had worked out for Max and Enzo.

"You need to keep an eye on Sofia. My father hinted that
going through you was the kinder way. And I want to get this
settled soon. When can you have the fake information planted
so I can hack in and steal it?"

"Tomorrow night," Enzo confirmed, a muscle pulsing in his
clenched jaw. "If Frank goes anywhere near Sofia, I'll finish him
off myself."

"No." That would complicate things. I couldn't let him even
entertain the idea. "We have a plan. Stick to it."

Emiliana

I paused at the entrance to Bramare's, the fine dining restaurant my family owned. Its happy chatter, clink of silverware, and familiar smells faded into the background as if it were white noise on a TV while a memory from shortly after Stefano had rescued me surfaced, and I let it play through my mind.

"It wasn't supposed to be this way," I'd said, resting my hand on his chest, over his heart so I could feel the reassuring beat. When we were young, I'd seen him, the tortured soul, the frightened little boy who soldiered on and put himself in harm's way to save his sisters and me.

He'd whispered that he was damaged and not worth it, but his gaze betrayed him and dropped to my lips. I closed the gap. I wanted to feel him too. He was becoming more and more a part of me. At the first touch, he lost control, but in a very good way. The desire and yearning present in the desperate way he kissed me turned my world upside down. I would never be the same, and I knew from that moment on that no one else would measure up.

"You're not broken." He pressed a kiss to my forehead, one of the only places not cut or bruised. "You're mine."

A tear had leaked from the corner of my eye. I was undone. With those two words, he'd helped to shield me against a mountain of evil. He didn't erase it, but I knew he loved me unconditionally, horror story and all.

Murmurs and a gentle nudge pulled me from the bittersweet memory, and I shook my head, freeing myself of the wayward direction of my thoughts when I heard Sofia's laughter and the clink of silverware in the restaurant where I was to meet her, Lil, and Eva. It was a good compromise for my overprotective brother that we chose to eat there. Of course, we all had guards scattered close by and around the restaurant in case anything happened. But if it did, I was ready.

The lack of clouds made the chilly fall day warmer and perfect for an outdoor lunch, so we sat in the garden area—I was tired of being cooped up in the house. I understood the safety factor and why my family, friends, and Stefano were so worried. But deep inside, that savage part of me awakened and wanted to come out and play. It bristled against my internal restraints.

"Hey!" Lil jumped up from her chair and hugged me. "Are you all right? I heard what happened yesterday."

Several heads turned, no doubt because of how stunning Lil was with her silvery-blond hair and blueish-purple eyes. All my friends were gorgeous. Lil was self-conscious, though, and didn't see what others did. Her cousin Eva intimidated her, and I'd never understood why. They were vastly different in appearance.

Besides, Max was crazy about her. That man only had eyes for his wife. It was sweet and something I dreamed of having someday—with Stefano. But he had such a tight rein on himself that I wasn't sure if that would ever happen. The few times his legendary control snapped had been the most erotic and all-consuming experiences I'd ever had.

When Lil released me and sat one seat over, I slid in between her and Eva. Sofia was across from me, smirking. Sofia knew what Lil had done, as she wasn't a fan of Eva. We both thought it was ridiculous. Eva was a lot, but for the most part, she was harmless.

They all stared at me, clearly expecting a response.

"What's going on in the fashion world?" I needed the focus off of me so I could breathe. I hadn't realized how stifling their concern was. Instantly, I felt bad. I shouldn't have reacted that way. The assholes were all dead, thanks to Stefano, Max, and my brother. My only wish was that I'd been able to get in on that action. There was a world of pain I would have loved to inflict on those men.

"It's crazy but fantastic. All I care about is getting my new line out for Fashion Week next year." Her whiskey-colored eyes always brightened when she talked about her career.

"Have you considered opening a boutique like our favorite shop? Or even having them carry your line?"

Sofia sipped on the mimosa put in front of her by a waiter who'd swept in and out with practiced ease. "I've thought about it but never pursued anything. It's a good idea, though."

"I could help you." Lil sat up straighter. "I have some time and could talk with Celia today. You could even have Enzo look into buying the boutique. It would be a good investment."

"And why the hell hasn't he already?" Eva waved over one of the waiters. She snapped the menu shut and, as soon as the waiter rushed over, placed her order.

We'd all eaten at Bramare's often and knew the menu by heart. I rattled off a soup and salad, then Lil and Sofia did the same. When the waiter was out of range, we launched back in to the topic of Sofia's new line.

"I've had calls about several high-end stores carrying every-thing, but I haven't moved on anything yet. I need to, though."

"It's something to think about." I didn't want to overwhelm her. She had my brother around, and I was sure he was doing his job in that department. I wanted to know what the other guys were doing. "What have Max and my brother said about who they think the rat is?"

"Frank." Sofia rolled her eyes. "He's the obvious choice."

"Well, yeah, especially since Antonio and Benito are out of the running." Lil grinned.

I flicked my thick braid over my shoulder—good riddance to both of the older Mafia bosses. Lil's father, Benito, had been horrible to her. There were times she was a shadow of herself because of how unloved he'd made her feel. Going away to college with us had been what she'd needed and where she'd shed the stigma he'd branded her with. Antonio, well… Nicole was better off. I had no idea about Tony, his second-born son. He hadn't done his firstborn, Max, any favors. No one felt remorse over Antonio's death, though we weren't sure about his business deals and were still finding things out long after his passing.

Tony was a wild card, the one we thought was the real information leak in the Five Families. Eva was with us, though, and she loved him for whatever insane reason.

A different waiter brought our food, and I thanked him.

"Have you spoken with Tony recently?" I asked Eva, doing my best to ignore how interested Lil and Sofia were. We all thought he was the rat, even though the guys had other ideas on the guilty party.

"No." She stabbed her salad. "I went to the club last night—"

"Which one?" Sofia interrupted.

"Temptation." Eva shrugged. "It was packed, and the line to get in wrapped around the building."

"That's great, though." Lil's voice was distant.

It was Max's club, and he'd put Tony in charge of that one at first. When he proved himself almost immediately, Max added Obsession, the second of the three nightclubs. Submission was the last one. It was dark and erotic, the one where the media thought illegal activity and danger happened. They weren't far off, but it was mostly clean. They all were, aside from the money laundering and whatever else the Caruso family ran through their legal businesses.

"Yeah, but he wasn't there. I spent so much time looking for him, and the staff wasn't any help. He must have been at one of the other clubs."

"Has anything changed between you two?" Sofia asked gently.

The unattainable-love situation had bonded Sofia and Eva months before when we'd all been at the lake house. Sofia had gotten her happily ever after, but Eva… well, she was in love with Tony, something I never thought possible.

"Not really." She stabbed more lettuce with her fork then let the utensil clatter against the plate. "I need to move on. I don't think Tony will ever see me as anything more than a fling."

"Then he's not worth your time. Don't give him any more of it." Lil pushed her half-finished food away, and a waiter cleared the plate from the table almost immediately.

"Are you sure he was at another one of the clubs?" It seemed odd. If the staff thought he was there, and he wasn't, that could have been one of the times he'd tried to cover his tracks while meeting with the enemy, whoever the enemy was—even though we all thought it was the Russians. It was too convenient that there hadn't been more retaliation after Ivan died. He was Yuri's underboss and eldest son, after all.

"No." Eva pouted, her features turning from speculative to miserable. "His staff was genuinely confused as they'd seen him earlier that evening. They said he would have notified"—she waved her hand in the air—"I don't know, someone. Maybe he was avoiding me and snuck out. He knows I wanted to talk, which was why I went there. He mentioned it was where he would be last night."

Sofia caught my eyes. Neither her, Lil, nor I trusted him. We needed to put a bug on him or something, find a way to track him but without Eva knowing—it would offend her if she thought we were eavesdropping.

"Why don't we go clubbing tonight? With all of us there, we'll corner him, and you'll be able to have your say." I couldn't believe what I was suggesting. Being in a room packed with people was going to be hell. Lil and Sofia would know that, though, and they would help. So would a lot of vodka.

Eva clapped her hands, her laugher loud and infectious. "I

love that idea! Let's do it. We can start with Obsession. It's fitting."

Sofia winked, her face angled so that only Lil and I could see. "Perfect. We'll go to Emiliana's to get ready around nine."

Eva threw her napkin on the table as a waiter approached. There was something different in the way he moved and in the hard glint in his eyes. Ren, the captain of my guard, must have noticed, too, because he pulled out his gun just as the waiter did.

Instead of shooting, the guy clipped Eva on the side of the head then lurched behind Sofia.

Eva slumped over, out cold.

Chaos erupted. Ren got a shot off that hit the waiter's shoulder before his body fell mostly behind Sofia. Her fingers curled around the knife on the table, and she thrust it behind her just as he pulled her to her feet.

Screams pierced the air as the diners around us became aware of what was happening. I blocked them out, focusing on Sofia and what I needed to do.

Lil and I launched ourselves after them with guns raised. I felt cold hard determination settle over me in an instant. He would not take her away. I would never allow it.

Two shots rang out, and the man released Sofia. He dropped to his knees, wavered for a second, then face-planted in a dead heap. Sofia turned and kicked him in the ribs. The guards swarmed us. Lil and I wrapped Sofia in a hug that didn't last long before she exploded at the guards.

"How the hell did this guy slip past you?"

One of the men stuttered, which only enraged her further as she jammed her index finger in his chest, and the large man's eyes went wide. It didn't matter that he towered over her. "I'll be having a strongly worded discussion about the hiring process with Enzo when I get home."

It was hilarious. Lil and I couldn't swallow the laughter, and soon, Sofia joined us. Our guards got us out of the open and into the restaurant. Once they combed the area and ensured no snipers were lying in wait, we would leave. One of them had picked Eva up and was checking her over from the clip to the temple she'd received.

I shook my head, meeting my friends' gazes. We would need to talk. Sofia had been the target, and we needed to know why.

CHAPTER EIGHT

EMILIANA

The talk with Sofia about why she was targeted never happened. Eva's wants took precedence when she insisted she was fine and that we go to the clubs so she could confront Tony. We went along with it and, later that evening, waltzed into Obsession, with its heavy thumping base and dark interior. The place was packed with people dancing and every available table and barstool filled. Lil and Sofia stuck close to me, as did our guards so that we had space to walk without anyone getting too close or bumping into us.

We climbed a few flights of stairs and wove down dark hallways, the sound from the first floor muffled. Word would reach Tony through the bouncers and security that we were here. I expected him shortly.

A door opened, and soon, we were in a large private box complete with a table and wraparound, u-shaped bench. There was a smaller dance floor and a bar in the corner with dedicated servers. The tension between my shoulders eased, and I took a deep, calming breath, accepting the drink Sofia was quick to procure. As I fell into a seat at the table, Lil joined me, and we chatted easily. We sat back to watch as the dramatics unfolded with Eva, content in our little section for the show.

Drinks flowed as we chatted and laughed, entertained by Eva. Later that evening, I motioned toward the bathroom, and Lil nodded then paused, turning her focus back to Tony, who had finally graced us with his presence. Eva distracted him enough for Sofia to slip his phone out of his back pocket without him knowing. She handed it to her guard, who then inserted the bug and gave the phone back to Sofia. Tony didn't notice the exchange, especially with the raging fight he and Eva were in, which showed no signs of letting up anytime soon.

The private box with its adjoining room equipped with a TV, bar, couches, and bathroom made this expedition bearable. When we'd entered and pushed our way through the thick crowd of people, I'd hovered on a full-fledged panic attack, and the itchy sensation still lingered. I needed a few minutes alone to regroup before going back in there and dealing with Eva and Tony's shit show.

The door separating both rooms from the hallway leading to the bathroom closed behind me, muffling the music to a manageable level. I pushed out a breath, shoving my hair away from my face. I was tired and wanted to leave, but Eva was nowhere near ready. *I could still go. Sofia and Lil will understand.*

Almost at the door to the bathroom, the hairs on my nape stood up, and I shivered—not from fear but awareness. Only one person could affect me that way. He changed the very air I breathed and had made me feel more alive than I had since the day my life went to hell. He must have moved because the heat from his body blanketed my side. I knew he would be there if I turned my head. My heart picked up as he leaned down, his lips brushing against the edge of my ear.

"What the hell are you four doing?"

I wanted to lean into him but held still. His knuckles brushed over my bare arm in a gentle caress. My head spun, dizzy with want. Any time he touched me or spoke in that low voice dripping with desire, I melted. Power, barely leashed strength, vibrated the air around him.

"Nothing." I didn't want to confess. The guys wouldn't let us do what we wanted. They were afraid and would follow us everywhere we went if they knew our plan to discover what Tony was doing, to prove he was the rat, while they followed up on whatever leads they had on Frank. "We decided to go out."

"Why don't I believe you?" His hand dropped to my hip, and he turned me, pressing my back against the wall.

In the dim light, the tenuous control that restrained him reflected in his eyes, and a muscle jumped along his square jawline. I was aware of how much he held back, that he was afraid to snap and unload the lust for me that shimmered beneath the surface. He thought I was fragile. In a way, I was, but not with him. I'd wanted him almost all of my life. I wouldn't let what had happened to me destroy what we could— what I knew we would—have if he would just let go.

Inch by inch, I let my gaze wander from the top of his dark-blond head, over his sinfully handsome face, to his broad shoulders, then to his chest. I pressed my palm flat against the hard muscles of his abdomen, exploring, traveling up toward his shoulders, and enjoying the way his body tensed beneath my touch.

I could feel his heart pounding, matching the frantic rhythm of mine. I was done. That stronghold he had on his emotions needed to snap. I wanted to feel all of him, and that was the only way I would.

The growl rumbling through his chest gave me a split-second warning of what was coming. I'd snapped his tenuous control. Excitement raced through me as he pressed me against the wall, holding my hands above my head in one of his. His lips found mine in a firm caress. I wanted it. Needed it. My mouth parted, and my tongue traced the seam of his lips. His hand clasped my hip, and he drew me close as he deepened the kiss.

I pushed against the hold he had on my hands, and he released me. I needed to touch him. Flush against his body, I could feel the hard press of him against me. I wound my arms around his neck, desperate to get closer, threading my fingers through his hair. With each sweep of his tongue against mine, heat built, and a pulsing throb built between my legs.

He moved his hand from my hip to cup my ass. With a little pressure, he lifted me off my feet, and I automatically wound my legs around his waist. He shifted so that my back was once again pressed against the wall, giving his hands the freedom to roam my body. I tasted the fiery burn of lust in the way he kissed me, and my body responded. Only he could do that to me. Anyone else would have left me cold, but with Stefano, it was never enough.

When he thrust his fingers through my hair to cradle the back of my head, I moaned from the sheer decadence of the way he kissed me. He pulled back, and his teeth scraped my lower lip before he trailed kisses from my jawline down to where my pulse beat frantically at the base of my neck.

Is this it? Will he finally move past kissing me? Because I wanted him to, and no one was in the other room, where there was a couch. *We could lock the doors. It could work.*

Wanting to take things further, to feel his skin against mine, I slipped my fingers between the buttons on his shirt then did the same with my other hand. Without hesitating, I yanked the two halves apart. Buttons flew off, clattering to the ground, and I feasted my eyes on his chest. A gasp escaped my lips and shattered the mood. I had expected to drool over his sinfully cut abs but what met my sight were overlapping rows of gauze across his chest and one shoulder.

His jaw hardened, and he pulled back, untangling my legs so

that they slid down his body. Once my feet were on the floor, he stepped back.

"What happened?" Tears swam in my eyes. He was everything to me, even though he didn't know it. I hated to see him in pain. And dressings like that meant his injuries were substantial.

He ran his fingers through his hair and looked to the ceiling.

I crossed my arms over my chest. "There's nothing up there that can help you. Please answer my question."

"Em, trust me. It isn't a big deal."

It was, or he wouldn't have minded me taking a look. "Okay." I moved closer and attempted to peek beneath the bandage, but he stepped back, and my hand met only air before I lowered it to my side. "If it's nothing, then show me."

"You need to leave. It's not safe here. That's why I came." He shifted his gaze away from me. "I'm sorry I let things get so out of hand."

I latched onto his hand with a grip so tight that he couldn't walk away, which I suspected he planned to do once he'd convinced me to go. "I wanted what happened between us. I've wanted that for a long time. With you. *Only* with you."

He met my gaze with determination.

Embers of heat seared me, and I wondered if my expression matched his. My traitorous body certainly did. If he hadn't pulled back, if I hadn't seen whatever injury hid beneath the wrap, we would have ended up in the private room on the couch. Part of me was glad we stopped, while the other half raged at the inconvenience of it all. "Come home with me." It was bold, and I knew that even if he didn't, the invitation would haunt him, testing his ability to resist. I wondered how long he would last.

"Not tonight. My father's been watching every move I make. If he sees me with you, you'll be a target for him to use against me. Trust me, neither of us want that."

I had to trust him. I wasn't comfortable around Frank, and

Stefano knew him best. If he said we needed to be careful, then we did.

"Before I found you here, I talked to Ren. They're waiting to take you home."

"Max owns this club. I'm probably safer here than at home." Not really, but I wasn't sure I wanted to leave. If Stefano was staying, I was too. I shoved my hair back, flicking the heavy weight over my shoulders.

He tracked my every move then shook his head. "I would feel better knowing that you're home. Enzo and Max are already on their way to get the girls out too. Please, Em."

I pushed out a breath. Giving in, I nodded. "Let me say good-bye, then you can walk out with me." Whatever was going down, I had to guess that it would be soon.

CHAPTER NINE

EMILIANA

The remainder of the evening was uneventful after Stefano escorted me from the club. I'd had enough time to hug everyone goodbye, and Sofia had whispered in my ear that it was done. They'd successfully bugged Tony's phone. I hoped we would have some proof of his disloyalty soon so we could cleanse the family and return to some normalcy.

Then there was Stefano. He was as frustrated as I was at our predicament. Frank worried him, and I suspected that the reason for the bandages had something to do with his father. I hated him. But I also knew how strong and almost inhumanly fast Stefano was when he fought. If he'd wanted to get out of whatever situation caused the injury, he would have devised a way... which meant he might not have wanted to. *Could he have been on a fishing expedition to learn more of Frank's dealings? Had he found anything out?*

There were too many things swirling around in my head, and none of them were peaceful. Eventually, exhaustion won, my eyes drifted shut, and I fell into a restless slumber.

The dream came without warning. I probably should have expected it, based on the night I'd had and the worry I'd seen in the guys' eyes when they herded my friends and me back to the safety of our homes, lending an air of impending danger. That was reason enough for my mind to dredge up the past and force me to relive the worst moments of my life.

It was dark. I was going out to meet my friends, and my car had already been brought around. The front door of my house slammed behind me, loud in the quiet evening, as I hurried down the steps to head out.

A fleeting thought skated through my mind that there wasn't a soldier waiting by the entrance, but I dismissed it just as quickly as it'd entered my head. I was almost to my car when I sensed movement behind me. Something dark and ominous closed in fast. All the hairs on the back of my neck stood up.

I pivoted, my foot hanging off the last step before landing on the driveway, mere feet from my car when my vision was blocked. My hands flew up, grasping at the hand at the back of my head that held the light-blocking hood in place. My nails clawed at my attacker's hand while I kicked blindly behind me in every attempt to dislodge his hold.

There was a sharp prick at my neck then burning at the injection site. The drug spread quickly, and my body refused to react to my frantic commands. I twisted, elbowed, and tried to throw my assailant off of me, but it'd happened too fast, and the drug spread through my system with disarming precision.

Each kick and punch was more ineffective than the last until darkness invaded to the point where I couldn't hold on any longer.

I gasped awake, the sensation of defeat a bitter taste in my mouth. I scanned my room, taking in the familiarity of it and the lack of intruders. A few deep breaths, and I shoved away the helplessness of what had happened all those years before. I focused on even, slow breathing, and the dream receded further.

As my awareness sharpened, I felt the comforting weight of

a gun in one hand, a knife in the other. They were never far when I slept, one under my pillow and the other secured where my bed touched the wall. An easy grab, which I had executed in preparation of what was to come. Thankfully, it was nothing.

My heart rate and breathing returned to normal, but the realization hit me that the past was too close and my subconscious was warning me that danger awaited and I'd better be prepared.

I set my weapons within easy reach on the duvet and grabbed my phone from the bedside table. The sun wasn't up, but the lightening sky foretold of the day's imminent arrival. My fingers flew over the keypad, texting Sofia and Lil in a group chat that we needed to keep a close eye on Tony. I felt that whatever was coming would be soon. We needed to stay on guard.

There was no answer from either of them, and I moved to sit, leaning against my headboard. I didn't expect them to be awake so early. Still, I wanted to talk to someone, to ground myself in connection and reassurance that I wasn't alone. The fact that Enzo and my parents had believed in me enough when I'd promised them repeatedly that I was fine and that they needed to live their lives rather than hover over me all the time said I was better. And I was. But they didn't know the extent of the monster that lived inside me. I'd let them see glimpses of it and of the intense fear that I'd never completely conquered. I was better, though, able to stand on my own. That was what they had seen when they'd agreed—the strength in my gaze, in my spine as I stood straight and faced each day with determination.

The nightmares came and went. I awoke to most of them with a silent scream inside my head, rather than vocalizing and shattering the peace of those around me. I was glad they'd thought I was healthy enough from the incident and had given me space to live my life. In turn, they did the same for themselves.

Only there was a part of me that was not okay, not by a long shot. My hands trembled as I waited for my friends to text me back and tell me that Tony was where he should have been, and not outside my bedroom door.

Even though I hadn't expected my friends to be awake, there was someone who was. We'd had a conversation once when I was broken and vulnerable, and he'd sensed it, choosing to sit in silence by my side one evening. He'd shared that he rarely slept, that the anticipation of being dragged from his bed as soon as he let his guard down was too real. He only managed four or five hours a night, tops, and it had been that way since he was a child.

My heart broke for him because I knew what he wasn't telling me. His father was the reason for his nightmares. Living in the same house, there was no escape. I wondered why he didn't leave.

My family was different, as was Sofia's. Lil's was in the same realm of awful as Stefano's. I hesitated for two seconds before quickly texting him, asking if he was awake.

Stefano: *Yeah. What's up?*

Me: *Bad dream. Felt like an omen.*

Stefano: *All's quiet here.*

Me: *K—thanks. Just thought I would check.*

He knew what my cryptic message referenced—safety. *Did he or any of the others learn who the rat was in our families?*

I would need an extra-long sparring session in my studio today. I tossed my phone onto my bed and did some stretches to get rid of the lingering stress and tension. Then I tightened every muscle in my body then relaxed, starting with my neck and working my way down to my toes. After that, I felt marginally better. My only hope was that no news was good news. Even so, I wished Stefano was with me.

CHAPTER TEN

EMILIANA

The fridge was open, and all I could think about was cooking a huge meal not just for myself but for about ten or more people. I needed to do something with my hands, to distract my mind, and cooking was my thing. Growing up, I'd loved helping my mom make sauce and, later, pasta. She taught me everything I knew.

That she and Dad were in Italy then traveling all over Europe for the next couple of months was a change Enzo and I were still adjusting to. Italians were all about family, and it was hard to see them move into retirement, but they deserved to enjoy time together without the constant worry of being in charge.

I glanced at the clock on the double oven. It was eleven, just enough time to get lunch started. I was going to cook for the soldiers patrolling the property. I needed something to do, and they could eat on their break. Ren could manage everyone. I would set the food up in the sunroom for when they had time to grab a plate.

It was my element. I poured a glass of wine, turned on music, and got to work on the sauce. Then I made the pasta.

The kitchen grew rich with the scent of meat, garlic, and tomatoes.

While the pasta was boiling, I got the long table set in the sunroom. A pitcher of ice water was next, and then I brought the salads. Freshly baked bread went on the other end. When the pasta was done, I drained it then tossed it in a pan with sauce. All that went in a large bowl in the center of the table. Instead of texting Ren, I went to the front of the house and out the door. I planned to ask the guard posted there to get the captain.

When I opened the door, I was surprised to see Ren standing there with Frank Rossi. All the tension that I'd worked so hard to get rid of rushed back. I refused to let him see it, though, and pasted on a wide smile.

"Mr. Rossi says he has an appointment with Enzo," Ren said, never taking his eyes off Frank.

It appeared that the captain didn't trust him either. Good judge of character. "Why don't you come in? I made lunch if you're hungry."

"That won't be necessary, but I would like to wait inside." He made a production of looking at his watch.

"Please, come in." I held the door wide.

As he walked past, cigar smoke trailed after him, and I fought from rubbing my nose against the smell. Ren was on his heels, and I was grateful. I stopped him with a hand on his arm long enough to tell him about the guards' breaks and food. He conveyed the message to the men then faded into the shadows so that he was there but not obvious.

Frank followed me into the kitchen, where I offered him a glass of wine. He declined. I knew he would. There was no way he was there to meet with my brother. Enzo wouldn't have forgotten or been late. No, Frank had something to say to me. Alone. And he was using Enzo as an excuse.

I'd maneuvered around the large island with the pretense of

getting him a glass of wine, knowing he wouldn't want one. It wasn't a social visit. He had a mission, and it didn't include my brother.

I waited for him to say something. Frank was ruthless. Whatever he wanted, he took with a brutality that stunned even the other bosses. Antonio had been cut from the same cloth, so vicious to his family that it was as if they were his pawns to move however he wanted. Their coldness was foreign to our Italian heritage.

"I came to warn you." His voice was low, guttural. "It's in your best interest to stay away from Stefano."

A shiver crept over me, but I hid it in movement, taking a sip of my wine. The Cabernet did its job, spreading warmth through my system. After setting the glass down, I met his gaze with what I hoped was disinterest. "Why would I be around Stefano?" That familiar darkness invaded my veins, and I pushed back at Frank. "Rather than playing whatever game this is, why don't you tell me the reason you're here? Because we both know it isn't to meet with my brother."

A spark of interest flared in Frank's eyes, and my blood boiled. I longed to palm a knife and slide it across his throat. The world would have been a better place without him in it.

I sensed Ren moving closer, but I had it under control. Frank wouldn't do anything to me. I leaned against the island casually while my other hand had a firm grip on the gun tucked into the waistband of the back of my jeans.

Frank's thin lips curved into a smirk. I wasn't fooled. He'd taken my measure and glimpsed the viciousness Italy had carved into me. He wouldn't underestimate me.

"Let me rephrase. If you distract my son from the life he is meant to lead, you'll find yourself back where he dragged you from, just as used and broken as before. But this time, you won't leave alive."

Motherfucker. I'd had enough. I drew my gun and leveled it at Frank, my finger on the trigger—ready. "Get out of my house."

Ren was at my side in an instant, his gun drawn as well. I could feel the fury vibrating from him. Frank's smirk fell away, and his eyes returned to the flat, dead expression he normally wore. The front door slammed against the wall. A second later, I caught a glimpse of Enzo's murderous rage as he barreled through the house and into the kitchen.

"Why the fuck are you here?" Enzo growled, the barrel of his gun drilling into Frank's temple.

"We had a meeting scheduled." Frank's hands hung by his sides, his posture unconcerned. "I was honoring it."

"That was scheduled for tomorrow at the warehouse."

Everything clicked into place for all of us. The meeting set for tomorrow was a front for his feigned miscommunication about the date and place to make his little venture look innocent. Too bad for him that Ren had also witnessed what Frank had said.

Enzo ushered Frank toward the door. They exchanged more words, but I didn't care what they said. The threat Frank issued was very real and proved that the guys might be on to something. If Frank had connections to make me disappear a second time, I needed to take his warning seriously. And I would. Instead of paralyzing fear, which would have happened even six months before, I felt white-hot fury. I would not let anyone take me unaware again.

Ren followed Frank out as the door slammed shut. He would ensure Frank left our property then beef up security even more. I put my gun back in my waistband. I should have been concerned, but I wasn't. So long as I remained vigilant, there would be no surprises. I would be safe.

In a blink, Enzo was in front of me. His hands gripped my forearms, and he bent so that we were at eye level. A blend of rage and fear swirled in his amber eyes. I pushed through the part of myself that was cold and dead, that would do anything to survive. It was hard, but I didn't want to worry him more than he already was.

Relaxing my shoulders, I offered a small smile. "I'm fine. Promise." The guys in my life were constantly asking if I was okay or not, and it was annoying. Sofia and Lil got it. They waited for me to tell them if I needed something. But we were close that way. I would go to them if I wanted to talk. The guys didn't know what the hell to do with emotions half the time. God forbid we cried. It freaked them out. And the worst part was that Stefano was the only person who centered me and made me feel completely safe. It killed my brother, but he understood. Stefano had carried me out of hell, leaving a bloodbath behind.

I couldn't rely on Stefano being there for me all the time, even though I wanted him with every fiber of my being. He was more than a savior. He was the man I loved, and I was tired of barriers keeping us apart.

The squeeze on my forearms brought me back to my brother's intense gaze, and I grinned, needing to reassure him that what I was thinking about was good. He would know I was lost in my head, but it wasn't anything traumatic that time.

Ren let himself back in the house before Enzo could question me about what that little sojourn had been. Enzo took a moment to study my expression. I was telling the truth, for the most part. Ren waited for us to break apart. When we did, he approached with the same fury that was written all over my brother's face.

"Frank Rossi threatened Emiliana." Ren didn't hold back as he gave Enzo the details of the conversation.

My brother pulled out his phone and called someone. "We have a situation." He motioned for Ren to stay with me while he went down the hall to his office when he was at the house.

When he was out of sight, I frowned at Ren. I hadn't planned to keep what Frank said to myself, but that was pretty damn abrupt.

"He needed to know." Ren didn't back down.

"I was going to tell him."

Ren's lips twitched as he fought a grin. "When was that? After you distracted him with all the food you made? Maybe some wine? And would you have given him all the details or softened it somehow?"

I rolled my eyes. "I don't need him moving home and dragging Sofia here too. They're starting their lives together, and—"

"You don't want your brother hovering and asking if you're okay twenty times a day?"

He got me. I winked then picked up my wine, waving for him to follow me to the sunroom. "I do not need that aggravation. Since you're in here, grab a plate." I handed him one then dished pasta onto it, forcing him to eat because I knew he'd let all the other guards but not take time for himself.

I sat with him while he ate, twirling the stem of my wineglass. "How am I going to convince my brother he doesn't need to move back?"

"This was crazy good." Ren polished off the food then put the empty plate and utensils in the bin I had at the end of the table for the kitchen staff to manage.

He leaned back in his chair, and I waited for him to tell me his thoughts. I'd known him all my life. He'd worked for my family for a long time, and we trusted him for more than his combat skills. He also had a good head on his shoulders and made quick, strategic decisions. "I don't think you're going to get out of this one. It's either going to be Enzo returning home, or—"

Ren stopped talking as movement caught my eye. Stefano entered the sunroom with Enzo. Both wore identical expressions. I couldn't stop my gaze from crawling over Stefano, that familiar sense of safety and uncontrollable desire a gut punch I wasn't expecting to experience that day. But there he was, and there I was, ready to leap into his arms… if my brother wasn't around. I stole a glance at Enzo. *Why does he look like he wants to hit someone then throw up?*

Ren got up with a mumbled excuse, the traitor. I made sure to shoot him a look of pure annoyance.

Once the three of us were alone, I sighed in resignation. It was clear they'd come to a resolution without my input.

CHAPTER ELEVEN

My fucking father had been alone with Emiliana. I wanted to do serious damage. The only thing holding me back was Enzo agreeing to my plan. Not willingly. He'd once threatened to shoot me, and if I hadn't pulled Em out of that shithole years ago, he would have. But that day would give me a free pass with him regarding his sister, something I exploited to get my way.

What I wasn't sure about was Em's reaction to what we'd decided, especially since she hadn't been part of the decision. But I was tired of hiding how I felt about her, and there was no way I would chance my father getting anywhere near her again. What he'd done had changed everything, and Enzo and I agreed. We would bring Marco and Max up to speed as soon as I got Emiliana out of there.

Em pushed past us and headed into the kitchen from the sunroom, where she had been with Ren. "If I'm going to entertain whatever it is you both think you're going to order me to do, I need some more wine."

I wanted to laugh because she was feisty as hell and not at all the broken shell Enzo and I had expected her to be after Frank's unnerving threat. Her long hair was twisted onto the top of her head in a messy bun, exposing her neck. I followed the sway of her hips then forced my gaze away before Enzo decided not to give me a free pass and shot me for checking out his sister. I wouldn't have blamed him if he did.

"Well?" Em refreshed her glass then looked wearily at her brother then me. "What did you decide without talking over with me first?"

Enzo winced. "I'm concerned for your safety. And it's either this or Sofia and I move back here, which I still think is the best-case scenario."

"We've been over that, and I already vetoed it. I don't need babysitting, and it's not fair to your relationship."

"You're moving in with me." Every muscle in my body tensed. I wanted it, and it was time to pull away from my father. I'd gotten everything I could from being under his roof, and I was so goddamned tired of being under his thumb.

"I'm sorry, what?" Em's brows furrowed, and she took a step back. "Why would I live in the same house as Frank? The goal was to stay the hell away from him, not decrease the amount of distance."

Enzo snorted, and I shoved his shoulder. I hadn't explained that well. "To my place on the lake. I'm going to stay there with you. The security is tight, and until we know who Frank could have on his payroll, one of us should be by your side twenty-four seven."

"Oh." Em lifted her glass then took a sip, studying me. "And you plan to be there all the time?"

"As much as possible. If I have to leave to conduct business, then Marco or your brother will be there."

"That seems a little excessive." She shifted her focus to Enzo. "You wouldn't do this to Sofia. I'm insulted that you both think so little of my fighting skills. I'm damn good with a gun and a knife."

"It's not that, Em," Enzo reasoned. "What if there are five guys next time? Yes, you're prepared, and it's unlikely you would be taken by surprise, but the number of people could be different. And hell yeah, I would do the same thing with Sofia. I am right now. Instead of Marco staying with her if I have to take care of something with one of the clubs, restaurants, or the bank, Max comes by with Lil. They're all in the same lockdown as you."

She pursed her lips, and I knew she would relent in the next second. When she gave a slow nod, I took that as agreement. "You need to pack. We're leaving here in an hour."

With a roll of her eyes, she left the kitchen. Enzo laughed then grabbed her wine and finished it in one gulp. "You have no idea what you're getting into. She's either going to cook everything in your house nonstop, want to spar, or binge-watch whatever new show she's found—with you."

He didn't get it. None of that was a hardship because I would be spending time with Emiliana. I'd wanted that since I hit thirteen and realized I had to stay away to keep her safe. It was a lesson my siblings and I had learned early on, and dismissing it would have led to life-altering consequences.

"It'll be fine." I left him there with a smirk on his face and went in search of Em.

I wandered the halls upstairs until I found her bedroom. I'd never been in there before. The walls were a rich blue-gray with accents of both light blue and gray. Her duvet was crème colored, and a throw rug tied all the colors together. She had a window seat and two large bookcases filled with books. There was a sitting area, a TV, and what looked like another room, her closet, where she was tossing clothes into a suitcase and muttering to herself. It was cute, and part of me didn't want to interrupt, but we needed to hurry.

"What can I help with?" I stepped into the closet, where she continued to toss clothes in the general direction of the suitcase.

"Can you take that suitcase"—she glanced behind herself and frowned—"and the clothes on the floor downstairs? I have to pack up some bathroom stuff, and I'll be ready."

I finished packing the suitcase while she rushed into the bathroom with another bag. It was so full that I had to plant a knee on the top so that it would zip shut. "I'll be downstairs. Let me know if you need me to grab any more bags."

"I'm good." Her disembodied voice floated to where I stood at the entrance to her room.

It was going a lot better than I thought it would. There wasn't any pushback from Em, and there could have been. She had a fierce temper at times. I backtracked until I was in the foyer, where Enzo leaned against the wall near the front door. I set the suitcase down then checked my phone.

"I'm still not sure about this," Enzo grumbled. "The only reason my sister is staying with you is that I know she would want to. It's a batshit-crazy idea, and you had better not take advantage of her, or I'll hunt you down and end you."

I arched a brow. I got it. She was his sister. I would have said the same thing, maybe worse. "You forget how I found her."

His face fell, and pain sliced through his brown eyes. "Fuck. Yeah, okay. I know you'll take care of her."

"Always." I glanced toward the stairs. "How long is she going to take?"

"Not as long as Sofia would."

As soon as he said it, Em appeared at the top of the stairs, laughing. "I heard that. If you don't want me to tell her, I guess you'll owe me something."

He pressed his lips into a line and said nothing. By the time she made it down the stairs, her laughter had died away, and the seriousness of what we faced hung heavily in the air.

"So Frank's the one? He fed me to the traffickers?" Naked vulnerability flashed across her face.

I balled my hands into fists as Enzo drew her into his arms. I had to stop myself from touching her, from reacting to her pain, but it wasn't my right—not yet. And Enzo didn't need to witness such things before I took his sister home to live with me.

"It's possible." Enzo hugged her until she pulled away. "I promise that we'll get to the bottom of this."

"I can't believe we had it wrong for all these years." Her voice was tight, controlled.

"We have to go." I grabbed both her suitcases while Enzo ushered her into my waiting car. After she was inside and the luggage was in the trunk, I turned to him. "Ren is coming?"

"Yeah. I would feel better if he's there."

"I'll let my captain know." Ren had been with them a long time and was loyal to the Vitale family. I wasn't worried about my father attempting to bring him onto his payroll. And I employed my own men, who were loyal to me, not my father. "It'll work out. I'll be in touch after I talk with Frank."

"When are you going to Frank's?"

"Tomorrow morning. I want to make sure Em is comfortable first, and I'll call and set it up with Marco so he can be with her while I'm gone." I slapped him on the shoulder then backed away toward the driver's side. "Try not to worry." I got in the car, shut the door, then turned to Em. "Ready?"

"Yeah."

Her purse was in her lap, seat belt in place. She looked sexy as hell, with her full lips painted a deep red. I started the car and drove down the long driveway. The drive would take about twenty minutes, depending on traffic.

My house was similar to Max's. It'd been mine for several years, and I went there whenever I could. A majority of the time was spent in my father's home for many reasons, mostly to get any information on him that I could. There was no love lost between us. I knew what type of person he was and how he thought of those in his family—we were pawns for his use. The man had zero emotion.

We drove in a comfortable silence, each of us processing in our own way. When we arrived at the secured garage under the four-story building, I parked near the elevator. Em didn't wait for me to open the door for her, so I grabbed the suitcases, shut the trunk, then rounded the car to join her. I keyed in the code, and the elevator doors opened.

She fidgeted with the strap of her purse. Aside from that, she seemed fine, but I wasn't sure, as she'd unwound her hair, and it curtained around her face, hiding her expression from view.

By the time the doors opened to the top floor, I was fighting myself to keep from sliding my fingers through her silky hair to move it away from her face. I didn't like it when she hid from me. After all we'd been through together, shutting down and not communicating wasn't going to work.

She stepped off the elevator, and the gasp that left her mouth told me she'd seen the view. The large windows took up most of the opposite wall, looking out onto Lake Michigan. It offered a sense of freedom, peace, and connection. After a moment, I motioned for her to follow me away from the open-concept kitchen and living area. The hall led to three bedrooms. I wanted her as close as possible and brought her to the one near mine.

"I thought this room would be better, but if you don't like it, you can use that one." I pointed to the other spare bedroom to the right. I wanted the most for her to stay in mine, but it was too soon for that.

"This is great. Thank you."

She smiled, and my gut tightened. It was going to be almost impossible to keep my hands off her. I cleared my throat, set her suitcases down inside the room, then backed out.

Enzo told me what he'd made for her after she'd returned from Italy, broken, a shell of the woman I'd once known and forever loved. Even with a battered body and bruised spirit, a core of steel shone in her dark eyes, screaming for retribution. There was no doubt in my mind she would return to herself, fiercer than ever. Her brother had empowered her, and in a few short weeks, she'd transformed, as I'd known she would. Not long after Enzo had built her a specialized private training room, I'd done the same in the basement floor of my lakeshore home for the day she would move in with me—I'd always thought she would.

"I have something to show you."

She tilted her head to the side, and a waterfall of dark hair fell over her shoulder. "You do?"

I couldn't wait to see what she thought. I took her hand and led her back to the elevator, minus the suitcases. When the door opened, we entered, and I pressed the button for the basement then tapped the code into the numbered panel to the right, giving us accessibility to the lower level. It was another measure of security.

"This feels very cloak-and-dagger." A grin tugged at the corners of her full lips, and I couldn't help but smile too.

"I added that so you wouldn't worry about anyone entering the space when you're down there." I told her the passcode so she could go down whenever she wanted.

The door slid wide to reveal the large open floor plan on the lower level below the garage. I flicked the switch for the strategically placed can lights that offered maximum brightness throughout as soon as we stepped out of the elevator. She gasped, tugging me with her. It was mostly open with wood floors and no windows. Knife dummies littered a portion of the room, and sandbags and tennis balls hung from the ceiling. I had automatic retractable panels where bags set on timers would drop down.

A rubber gym floor designated the weight room that held all my equipment in the opposite corner, including a punching bag and two treadmills. Along the far side of the wall from where we stood were a full bathroom and wet bar. I hung back as she explored, warmth filling my heart at how happy she appeared.

"This is amazing. I love it. And I can use it whenever I want?" She spun around, her bottom lip caught between her teeth and excitement sparkling in her near-black eyes.

"I designed it for you." I closed the distance between us, my hand resting on her hip as I drew her forward. I couldn't resist touching her. "After I saw what Enzo built you, I did something similar. The gym was already here, but I added the section for you to train with your knives. If you look in the credenza, you'll find a range of real and rubber knives."

I released my hold on her so she could go check out the weapons. When she lifted the top of the cabinet to reveal the display within, she sucked in a breath then grasped a dagger with a red handle wrapped in crisscrossing-patterned black leather, allowing portions of the red to show through.

"Stefano, these are beautiful."

I came up behind her, wrapping my arms around her waist as she admired the various weapons. "They're all yours."

She replaced the knife and lowered the lid. Then she turned and looped her arms around my neck. Tears of happiness swam in her eyes. "Thank you. I can't even tell you how much this means to me."

"You don't need to. I understand you on every level and know how important this is."

She licked her bottom lip, her gaze dropping to my mouth.

I couldn't deny the invitation and brushed a kiss across her lips, not intending to deepen it until hers parted. There was no way I could resist Emiliana when she opened for me. Tasting her was an addiction, one I planned to indulge in for the rest of our lives.

Desire swept through me with the swiftness of a brush fire. I slowed the kiss, attempting to regain control of my need for her. When I broke the kiss and eased back, my gaze roved over her swollen lips and dilated pupils. I forced myself to put space between us and clasped her hand in mine. I wanted this with her more than anything, but she'd just arrived, and I didn't want to overwhelm her. She let me lead her back to the elevator, and we rode to the top floor in silence. When we entered the living room, I squeezed her hand before releasing her, wanting her to have a few moments to adjust and get comfortable with her new home. Unable to stop touching her, I cupped the side of her face. She leaned in to my touch, and my pulse kicked up a beat.

"I'll let you get settled. I have a few calls to make, then I thought we could watch a movie or sit on the balcony, maybe eat dinner out there?" My hand fell away, and I missed the feel of her soft skin instantly.

"That all sounds great. I'm going to change first, but can I poke around in your kitchen?" Her cheeks pinked becomingly.

"You don't have to ask. While you're here, this is your home too." What I meant was that I didn't want her to ever leave.

CHAPTER TWELVE

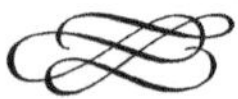

EMILIANA

I changed into yoga pants and a loose, extra-soft, long-sleeved tee. Comfort was the goal of the evening. It was strange to be in Stefano's lakefront home. It reminded me of him with its modern vibe of dark and light gray, white, and a blue that I was in love with. And then there was being there with him and no prying eyes. I couldn't have dreamed up a better situation. If my brother had known there was more to how Stefano and I felt about one another or anything about all the stolen kisses, he would never have agreed to the arrangement. Enzo saw how Stefano's presence comforted me but missed the frustration and painful awareness that went hand in hand with that. Besides, he was so wrapped up in Sofia that I was able to hide a lot of what I felt about Stefano.

The thing was, we weren't supposed to be together. My family wanted me to stay far away from Stefano because his relationship tied me to Frank. He could protect me, sure, but nothing more. They worried about Frank Rossi with good reason—he had found and would find any way to keep us apart. After our disturbing conversation earlier that day, I had grown sure he'd had a hand in turning me over to the traffickers. And I would have freaked out, but the excitement and security of being in Stefano's private home helped to keep that at bay.

I wandered out to the balcony. It was large enough for a couple of lounge chairs, a small table, and a grill. It was chilly. I was glad I had long sleeves but would have welcomed a blanket to shield me from the wind coming off the lake. I popped back inside and grabbed the throw from the couch. Stefano hadn't come out of whatever room he was making calls from, so I got comfortable on the terrace. The rhythmic sound of rolling waves lulled me, further calming me.

Twisting my hair so that it lay over one shoulder, I snuggled into the blanket and kicked my feet onto the ottoman, watching the clouds thicken and roll. A storm was coming. It matched the day's mood. By the minute, the sky darkened, and the wind picked up.

I knew I could get used to the beauty and freedom of where his home was located. Waves grew in height, whitecaps dotting the water. A dark line moved forward where the storm raged, still miles away on the horizon. Even so, I couldn't bring myself to go in.

It wasn't long until I heard a door open then shut somewhere inside as Stefano made his way to the living room. Sparks of awareness traveled through my limbs when he stepped onto the balcony. I turned my head so I could look at him, tucking my hair behind my ears to curb the wind from dancing with the long strands.

Electricity charged the air, and I was unsure whether it was from the pending storm or the attraction between us. All the fine hairs on my body stood on end, and restless anticipation skated down my spine. He towered over me, and my mouth went dry.

God, he was beautiful. I skimmed over his piercing eyes then along his angular cheekbones, slightly crooked nose, and strong jaw. I didn't dare check out anything lower. He'd already caught me doing that once today, and we had things to talk about, even though I would rather lose all my inhibitions.

I fought the urge to stand before him, rise onto my toes, and kiss him. I knew he would react—one touch, and we combusted. So much pent-up need and emotion existed between us. I wanted so much from him, but I wasn't sure what he could give while he was deep in the process of uncovering Frank's schemes.

Lightning flashed a good distance out, and not long after, thunder rumbled in response. Stefano sat in the chair next to mine, shifting so that he faced me. Maybe he liked the atmosphere too. We both battled things beyond our control, and the storm reflected the inner turmoil so well.

He leaned forward, elbows on his knees, and I longed to run my fingers through his dark-blond hair then along his stubbled jaw.

"I don't want to make you feel like you're trapped here, Em, but it would be easier to keep you safe if you didn't leave unless you were with one of the other bosses or me."

I nodded in agreement. It was a small concession, and I was where I'd wanted to be for so long—alone with Stefano.

He thought I was fragile, and he was afraid to act on how he felt. I was so tired of that. It was my chance to break down those walls. He'd kept me at a distance for so long. The only time he'd let me in was when he'd rescued me. I would never forget how hard he'd fought and how he'd treated me as if I was the most precious thing in his world. From that one glimpse, the raw emotion that burned within him blazed, and I wanted more.

"Why now?"

"Because I can't fight how I feel about you anymore." He took my hand in his, toying with my fingers. "I don't want to push you into something you don't want. I only know that I can't stay away from you in an attempt to keep you safe."

"I can take care of myself."

"That's not what I'm saying. There are things you don't know. My father has threatened your safety and my sister's too many times to count. I stayed in that house to protect both of you. This last time wasn't just a way to make me compliant—my father went to you directly. That changes things, and there is no way I'll leave you alone to face what he's capable of."

"I want us to be honest with one another." Time was short. Both of us knew that too well. "I want more."

A predatory stillness settled over him, and if I hadn't known him as well as I did, it would have been terrifying. But I knew what I was to him, even if the rest of the world didn't. He'd showed me in so many ways—how he kissed me, in the way he touched me, how he defied his father, and in the river of blood in the wake of rescuing me.

"Not just to be here with you as friends. We've danced around the attraction between us, keeping it to the shadows and away from our family and friends for years. I don't want to do that anymore."

He got up, desire swimming in his hooded eyes. Then he was at my side, gathering me in his embrace. He settled on the lounge chair with me lying on top of him, his arms holding me in place. Neither of us said anything, but we didn't need to.

***

I'd fallen asleep in the guest room he'd given me. It wasn't where I wanted to be, but we were feeling our way into taking our relationship a step further, and I was all right with that. Sleep came swiftly. And as the storm raged outside, so did the ones in my memories, invading my dreams with brutal force.

It felt like drowning. Something horrible was happening, but I was a prisoner in my mind. Too many feelings penetrated the walls of euphoria where I existed. My breath hitched on a gasp as agonizing pain radiated from every cell. I clawed my way to reality with desperation, trying to scrape together enough calm in the invading horror of my situation to fool my captors. I needed to escape, to find any opening I could, and get out of the putrid bed that smelled of sweat, blood, and bodily fluids I didn't want to connect to the acts being done to me against my will.

They controlled me with drugs. I wasn't the only one. I could hear the other girls. They were mostly in makeshift cubicles with mattresses thrown on the ground, sheets dividing one from the next. A parade of men filtered through that house of hell. In those brief moments of clarity, like the one soon within my grasp, I'd killed: a broken spine, the perfect strike to the front or back of the neck. I wanted more of that and fought the effects of the drugs. The only reprieve came when the asshole on duty got lazy and let the opioid doses lapse enough for my mind to be my own again.

The next time he or any other man who thought he could take what wasn't his came in, I would end him brutally. That was what I lived for. I didn't focus on rescue. My family would search for me and come, but I would do maximum damage and look for every opportunity to break free.

I blocked the shame, the way my body hurt in unimaginable ways, and the sheer desperation so that I could focus on one breath then the next. The drug had left my system slowly, along with the hold it had on me. The sense of relaxation, the ability to block pain through its false world, loosened. Breathing was easier. Soon, strength would return to my limbs. I took stock of anything new from the last time I was lucid.

Zip ties cut into my wrists. My arms were secured to a bedpost above my head. They'd moved me from a mattress on the floor to one with a frame, with a metal headboard to secure me. One ankle was tied to the opposite end of the bed. There were no sheets, nothing to use to choke my victim. And there would be one. I would kill the next person who came in, or die trying.

Someone entered. My mind shied away from what happened next. A high-pitched alarm pierced my groggy state as my world spun and shook.

"Emiliana!"

I jerked awake. My fist aimed straight for the large figure looming over me, who blocked my strike. Blind panic fueled me, and I lurched upright to headbutt him. He shifted at the last second, swearing before strong arms banded around me and soft words filtered through the haze of desperation.

"It's Stefano. You're okay. Come back to me, Em."

I turned my hands to grasp his arms, waiting for the shaking to stop. As soon as I found the words, I told him I was all right. He swept me into his arms then lifted me. We were moving. I closed my eyes and sank into the security his embrace offered. He placed me on another bed, and I jerked upright. I didn't want to be alone. The memories were too close.

"You're in my room. I'm not leaving you." He got back in bed, drew me into his arms, and pulled the covers over us.

I could breathe easier, the nightmares chased away by his presence. It was where I was meant to be and where I would fight to remain.

CHAPTER THIRTEEN

EMILIANA

I snuggled against the heat rolling off Stefano, content to lie in his arms for another few minutes. Light streamed through the windows, and the sound of the waves filled the bedroom. The room was chilly, as he'd cracked the sliding glass door open. It was October in Chicago and getting cold, especially along the lake.

Stefano pulled me closer so that my cheek rested on his chest, and I sighed. In his arms, I felt protected and safe. He kept the nightmares at bay, and since he'd brought me to his room, I planned to stay in his bed. Remaining under lock and key in the building wasn't ideal and something I would have to talk about with him.

"Morning." His voice was gruff and sexy as hell. "Did you sleep okay?"

"I did, and I'm sorry about waking you the way I did." I was grateful that he couldn't see my face. My cheeks were hot, and I was drowning in embarrassment. I knew why the dreams were back. The threat from Frank was a huge trigger, and I couldn't let myself dive into what he'd insinuated, at least not for the time being.

Stefano ran his fingers through my long hair in a soothing rhythm. "I won't let anything happen to you."

I wasn't the only one the dreams had tormented. From the tone of his voice, my scream last night had resurrected the memory of when he found me. Our lives were bound from childhood and again that fateful day in Italy. We weren't supposed to be together, but nothing ever felt so right.

The years fell away, replaced by the dark interior of Stefano's childhood home and the time I'd left Marissa's room when I shouldn't have, in search of Stefano. But I wasn't the only one who had found him.

"What do we have here?"

My body trembled from the sound of the hoarse voice, and I stepped back, my shoes hitting the wall. There was nowhere to go. Stefano edged slightly in front of me, trying to block me from his father. The man scared me. All the bosses were dangerous, but he was something else, too—evil. While Sofia's dad was terrifying, it was never to us. Same with my dad. But Stefano's father didn't like us, and we knew we weren't entirely safe around him.

"She was looking for the kitchen, for a glass of water. I was going to show her where it was." Stefano moved a few more inches so that I was almost hidden behind him.

His father growled. "You have a job to do."

I closed my eyes tightly and curled my fingers into the fabric of his shirt, wishing I was back by my mom in the other room with my friends.

"But Drago's there. I thought—"

A loud crack sounded. His shirt ripped from my grasp, and I gasped. Stefano was on the ground, his father looming over him. I tried to make myself small, but Mr. Rossi wasn't even looking at me. He shook his finger over his son, his face red with anger.

"You're not to think. Do as you're told. Go back to the basement. Now." His gaze swung around, and my knees knocked together. "Get the hell out of here unless you want the same treatment."

I ran back in the direction I'd come, tears streaming down my face. As my heart broke for Stefano, the connection I felt for him shifted. It strengthened, and I knew we were forever bound.

I snapped out of the memory to the soothing motion of Stefano's fingers running through my hair. He never pressured me for anything more, even though I knew he would have liked to take things further. But he'd seen me at my worst, and I think it scarred him on a similar level. When we ventured into more than a physical relationship, and we would, it would have to be because I initiated. It would have been strange behavior for such an alpha male if our history hadn't been there. But it was, and it was a giant wall without footholds.

His abs tightened, distracting me as he pressed a kiss to my forehead. When he had taken me from my bed to his the night before, I'd only glimpsed the black boxer briefs he wore, outlining his body to perfection. I wanted to explore every inch of him, but for the time being, I was okay with being held. I think we both needed it.

My phone chimed from the other room. I'd never turned the volume down, and the sound carried. Then Stefano's did too. He sighed and reached for it, typed in a response, then physically lifted me so that we were sitting.

"Marco will be here in a half hour."

"You're going out?" He wasn't wearing the bandages any longer, and as he leaned forward and scrubbed his hands over his face, I got my first glimpse of his back, and my heart broke. "Stefano."

He grunted then shoved the covers back, but I grabbed his forearm. I'd always known his dad was a monster, but I wasn't sure why it was still going on. Stefano could have overpowered him. Even though my perception had been hazy in Italy, I'd seen the carnage he'd left to get to me and take me from that place.

When his head swung in my direction, the bleakness of his eyes pierced my heart. I draped a leg over him so that I straddled him. Cupping his face, I pulled myself up enough so that our gazes locked and held. "What happened?"

"It's nothing for you to worry about."

Fierce protectiveness flooded my system, heating everything in its wake. "Of course I'm worried. I know what made those marks."

He said nothing.

"Frank did that, didn't he? Why?"

He pulled my hands from his face and sank his fingers into my hair, drawing me close. When his lips brushed over mine in the lightest of touches, I melted into him. Then he pressed our foreheads together. "Sometimes, it's good not to show all the cards. I need information from my father, and I'll do what I have to get it."

The rumble of his quiet voice sent a shiver racing along my spine. "And did you?" I rested a palm over his heart, feeling the steady beat.

"Enough to know that he's working with the Russians."

"He told you that?" That meant, beyond a shadow of a doubt, that he was the rat—one of our own, from within the family. If his betrayal was true, he was a dead man walking. Nothing would save him.

"No." A muscle along his square jaw jumped. "He didn't have to. It was clear in the order I was given."

I jerked back, severing the connection where our foreheads touched. "What order?"

He lifted a strand of my hair and then twisted it around his finger. "Nothing to worry over. I've already met with Max and Enzo."

"With two of the bosses, but not Marco? Why not him?"

"He'll be brought into the loop soon. Max has an idea of how to get Elena back that involves Marco. I'm only telling you this to emphasize how important it is that you stay where I can protect you and far away from my father."

I nodded absently. I hadn't planned on going anywhere near Frank. But what Stefano hinted at conveyed a new level of hell that would affect us all if we didn't do something to stop him. A tremor ran through my body, and the familiar bloodlust followed in its wake. I wanted to be the one to deliver the death blow.

The grip on my hips changed, and I blinked Stefano back into focus. The intensity in his gaze caused me to gasp. He knew what I was thinking, and I saw an answering brutality within him that sang to my damaged soul.

"We're in this together, Em. You trust me?"

"I do." He'd proven himself to me repeatedly since we were kids. My faith in him was unshakable.

He tucked the strand of hair he'd been toying with behind my ear then trailed his fingers down my cheek until he cupped the back of my neck. "I promise that I'll bring you in on everything soon. I need a little longer to slip the noose around his head."

"Don't take too long." My hungry gaze skimmed over his body in a visual caress. "And don't let him lay a hand on you again."

A wolfish grin flashed across his face before he dropped his feet to the floor then lifted me to my feet as he stood. He held me at arm's length as anticipation buzzed through me. I didn't dare breathe. Then he spun me around so that my back was to him.

"Go get dressed." He smacked me lightly on the ass. "Marco will be here in a matter of minutes, and I'd prefer not to have to kill him if he sees you walking around like that."

I laughed as I hurried to my room. I was wearing light-pink

boy shorts and a tight sleep shirt, hardly scandalous. It only took me a few minutes to take a shower, brush my hair and teeth, and get dressed and throw my hair into a high ponytail. I wanted to make something for breakfast. Maybe omelets. I could do scones too.

Stefano was already in the kitchen when I got out there. The sleeves of his black button-down shirt were rolled up, showcasing strong forearms, and my mouth went dry. The rich aroma of coffee filled the space and lured me closer. I took a seat at the island as he set a mug in front of me. With a heavenly sip, I watched him over the rim.

When he joined me with a steaming cup, his phone pinged, and I remembered that mine had a while ago, but I'd never looked at it. Lil and Sofia had texted that they were coming with Marco.

I took another couple of sips, and after finding out that Stefano wasn't hungry, decided to make scones. I gathered the ingredients, preheated the oven, and got to work making them. It wasn't long until the sweet scent of blueberry pastries added to the rich aroma of coffee.

Stefano sent the elevator down to let everyone up then took off, saying he would be a couple of hours. After Marco said hello, he disappeared into Stefano's office to take care of a few things. Sofia threw her waist-length faux-fur coat on the back of the couch. Her long, wavy hair was up in a high ponytail like mine, while Lil's eye-catching blond hair hung down her back. She'd worn a sweater without a coat and carried two champagne bottles. I grinned as I took both from her.

"You have orange juice, right?" Sofia frowned. "I didn't think to ask since Stefano told me he'd made sure the kitchen was stocked for whatever cooking whim you wanted to follow."

I rolled my eyes. "Please. You know you love it when I cook."

"Well, yeah." Sofia grinned.

"And by that sweet smell, it looks like we'll be the happy

recipients." Lil laughed as she popped one of the corks from the bottle. "Grab the OJ, Sof."

"On it!"

The timer beeped, and I took the scones out to cool while Sofia grabbed glasses then poured orange juice. Lil followed with the champagne then handed them out. We clinked glasses, and warmth filled me. Not from the drink, although that was great, but because my best friends were there.

"So"—Sofia hopped onto a barstool—"spill."

"Spill what?" I feigned confusion.

"Come on." Sof looked to the ceiling as if there were answers there, causing Lil to choke on her drink. "You've been into him since we were little."

"Kind of like you and Enzo?" Lil's cheeky comment procured an eye roll from Sofia.

"First of all—*ew*—that's my brother, so no details, please. And nothing happened with Stefano and me. Not really."

Both of their expressions fell, but I wasn't going to tell them my nightmares were back. Besides, nothing had happened.

"But you're hoping to change that?" Lil got up, opened and closed cabinets until she found a pitcher, then got to work on making ready-to-pour mimosas.

I took a sip of my drink then arranged the scones on a plate and set it between us. "Yeah, I do. And I think the timing for us is right, so long as our world doesn't implode, and we all know that's likely."

"Agree, but it shouldn't cause an issue between you and Stefano." Sofia grabbed a scone. "So let's figure out what we're doing with Tony. Lil and I have been monitoring him. There's not a lot to report though, except—"

"That he's avoiding Eva." Lil winked at Sofia as she reached for a scone too. "Twice when she went into one of the clubs, he got the hell out of there fast. I have no idea why."

I downed the rest of my mimosa, thanking Lil when she

poured more. "I thought they had something going on, or at least it seemed like they were on an even playing field this time around. Before, Tony was all about power and being boss of one of the families, and now, he runs two of the Caruso family clubs."

"That's what we think is weird too," Sofia said. "Eva is hot. There is no way Tony isn't into her."

"Or maybe that's the thing. I'm almost positive they had something going at one point. It could be that he's just not into her anymore," Lil said.

"We should keep watching him, to be sure, but I don't think it's Tony who's the rat."

"What? Since when did you change your opinion about Tony?" Lil's stare remained steady on me.

I leaned close so that Marco wouldn't hear anything if he came out of the office while I was telling them what had happened with Frank. "You guys know that Frank threatened me, right?"

"This is new information." Lil's eyes were wide, and her skin was paler than usual.

Sofia's lips were pressed into a straight line, and she gave a jerky shake of her head. "No. Enzo failed to share that little detail. Do tell what the asshole said to you."

I gave them a recap, including how it had seemed as if he was the one behind my being taken and turned over to the trafficking ring in the first place.

"He needs to die." Sofia slammed her drink back, downing it in one gulp. "Let's go pay him a visit."

Lil grabbed my hand in a tight squeeze. "We need to do something. This can't go unpunished."

"You're right." My voice held steel. I would not be a victim again. "And he will. The only problem is that I promised Stefano I would let him handle things, at least for now. He needs information from Frank."

"Are you sure you can wait?" Lil asked, tears misting her eyes.

"I'll have to. I trust him with my life, and if he's asking me to do this, I will." I hoped it wouldn't be too long, because the nightmares sucked. Although with their return, Stefano wouldn't want me to sleep anywhere but with him, which wasn't a hardship in any way.

Sofia and Lil stayed a few more hours, and Marco joined us once he'd finished working. It had always amazed me that he was Sofia's older brother—his green eyes and black hair were completely different from Sofia's amber irises and mahogany tresses. Still, they acted like siblings in how they teased each other, and they were fun to be around.

Not long after Marco managed to finish the last scone, Stefano walked through the door. I couldn't stop my heart from racing and butterflies from taking flight in his presence. I swore he only had eyes for me as he came over and stood inches from where I leaned against the island. Sofia read the room and hurried everyone out. I hugged her and murmured "thanks" as they got into the elevator. Then I was left alone with Stefano and suddenly nervous about it in the most compelling way.

CHAPTER FOURTEEN

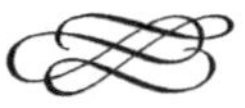

STEFANO

I couldn't take my eyes off Emiliana when I stepped off the elevator. It was a damn good thing her brother wasn't there, which was surprising. Enzo didn't want Sofia out of his sight, especially given the information I'd shared with him and Max about Frank's order to extract Elena's address from Sofia if need be.

Marco and the girls left, and I barely stopped myself from shoving them out faster. I wanted to be alone with Emiliana. Her long, dark hair was pulled into a sleek high ponytail that swung when she moved around the kitchen, cleaning up the plates and glasses from earlier.

Something smelled incredible, and my stomach growled. Em laughed as she turned at the sound, her eyes sparkling with mirth, and I had an image of her in the future, laughing, cooking, and always by my side. I wanted that with her, and I knew I would do everything in my power to make sure we had that. I just needed a little more time to find out who Frank's connection was in the family—there had to have been someone else. Too many vital pieces of information, which my father couldn't have gotten himself, had leaked and put those I loved in jeopardy. It would not happen again. The rest of his informants would be found and dealt with accordingly.

"Do you want a sandwich?"

Em's question drew me from the turn my thoughts had taken. "That would be great." I reached around her for a bottled water as she pulled out bread, sandwich meat, and various other items. "How were things with Sofia and Lil?"

"Good." She arranged everything on the cutting board and got to work with the tomato and lettuce. "We had a lot of fun. I needed that today."

"They can come over anytime." I meant it. As she moved around the kitchen, I caught a whiff of the light, airy perfume she wore, and my gaze dropped to her neck. I wanted to run my lips over the sensitive skin there, feeling her pulse flutter beneath my touch. When she set the plate in front of me, I grabbed a seat and took a bite. So good. I'd devoured almost all of it while she put everything away then sat next to me.

"How did everything go? Did you find anything more about Frank?"

"No. I was with Enzo. We're working on a false lead to give to my father." I polished off the rest of the food then got up and put the plate in the dishwasher. "Do me a favor, though."

"Of course." She rested her elbows on the island and smiled.

"Don't tell the girls or anyone else what I've told you. We need to keep the information close until Frank buries himself and incriminates any others he's working with. Especially if they're in the family, which I suspect they are."

"I won't." Her teeth sank into her bottom lip, drawing my notice.

"It's not too cold out, and the wind is hardly blowing for once. Do you want to go on the balcony for a while? I have an hour before I need to make calls and check on things for the family."

She nodded, and I opened the accordion doors and ushered

her outside with a hand on the small of her back. She went to sit on one of the chairs, but I had other ideas and pulled her into my arms then got comfortable on one of the loungers. She snuggled against me, tangling our legs as I spread the throw over us.

Emiliana

The ever-present sound of the waves below added to the ambiance on the terrace. I rested my cheek on Stefano's chest while he ran his fingers through my hair. "How did the meeting go?"

"It went well. The false lead that Enzo and I created will be in my father's hands by tomorrow morning."

"And will that end his hold over you? Will we have evidence on him to justify retaliation in the eyes of all the bosses?"

"It could be the catalyst for what we'll need."

His body was tense as he talked about his father, but I needed the information. I would not be left in the dark. "Do you regret leaving your home because of me?"

With a finger beneath my chin, he tilted my head back so that our eyes met. "I would do anything for you, including finding a way to entice you to live with me when you're ready." His thumb slid over my bottom lip in a slow caress. "You're mine. I've thought of you that way since we were kids, but if I selfishly acted on my feelings, I couldn't protect you from him."

My heart warmed. "I would have come to you long ago if you'd let me know." *So much wasted time.* "I don't want to go back to my room." I let everything I was thinking show in my expression. That was it. That night, we would bridge the gap that still existed between us and solidify that we were together. There was no one else for me and never had been.

Attraction and sheer need crackled between us before his mouth was on mine, coaxing my lips to open. My fingers grazed his stubbled jaw then trailed lower to spread over his tight abdomen, and I felt his quick intake of air. Our clothes melted away, the need for skin-on-skin contact undeniable. We stretched out on the lounge chair, his body partially covering mine and the chilly air swirling around our heated bodies.

With Stefano, I was safe and free, and he would show me a world that offered so much more, where no remnants of past experiences existed.

"Em," he said as he peppered kisses along my jaw to the top of my breast, hovering over my heart before he looked up and met my gaze. Desire flooded his brown irises to almost black, and I shivered in anticipation of the dark promise swirling in them. "You're so beautiful. I love you, always have."

I cupped the side of his face, tears misting in my eyes. "I love you too. You're the only one for me."

His shoulders flexed as he returned to my body, trailing kisses over my breasts and abdomen then shifting so that he spread my legs until I was bared to his hungry gaze. My fingers twitched with the need to explore the well-defined contours of his body, but for the time being, I was at the mercy of his ministrations.

Then his mouth was on me, and I lost all train of thought as sensations flooded my body. His tongue pressed against my clit, pinging electricity through the sensitive bundle of nerves. Heat pooled low. When he eased a finger inside, moving with the rhythm of how he tongued me, I arched, gasping as a wave of pleasure crested then crashed through me. My body quivered beneath his touch. I couldn't have held on even if I'd wanted to.

He crooked his finger, added a second, and increased the friction on my clit, and my body exploded. I arched into him as I fell over the edge.

But he was there to catch me. When he climbed up my body

with a predatory gleam, I welcomed his weight, purring in delight.

I felt the hard press of him settle between my legs. Then his lips found mine, brushing back and forth, stoking the embers of my desire all over again. With each caress, I quivered with need, melting against him. I moaned as he deepened the kiss, and my hands rested on his shoulders, exploring the contours as the muscles shifted and bulged. My body hummed, my need escalating and hypersensitive to his every touch.

Heat pooled low in my core, and I felt myself softening, readying for his entrance. I met his burning gaze then arched beneath him, urging him to move.

He rested his forehead against mine. "Are you sure, Em?" His voice, deep and husky with desire, held so much promise.

Need and want sizzled through me. "I want you, Stefano. I'm sure."

As he eased the tip of his length deeper, my core infused with heat, slicking the way for his entry. I pushed back against him, insisting he move. Then his mouth claimed mine in a heated kiss, urgent and demanding. When he plunged inside, I exploded around him in earth-shattering convulsions.

My fingers traced over the corded muscles in his back as they flexed and bulged beneath my touch with each powerful thrust. When he broke the kiss, I whimpered, but he trailed heated kisses along my neck, scraping his teeth where my pulse fluttered wildly. Sensations built in cresting waves, and my head swam. I was close, teetering on the edge. Then his fingers dipped between our bodies, and he brushed over my sensitive bundles of nerves. I cried out, my body convulsing around his.

He pumped into me, chasing my climax until he fell over the edge with a moan. I welcomed the solid weight of him as we lay together, waiting for our heartbeats to regulate. I clung to him, my legs still wrapped around his waist, shaken by what I'd experienced.

Neither of us moved until he noticed the goose bumps traveling up my arms. Intense emotion burned in his eyes, and I knew mine looked the same. When he pulled out and shifted to the side, I felt empty.

He gained his feet then tugged me to him. "Let's go inside where it's warm."

I brushed his mussed hair back from his forehead, leaned against him, and smiled. We went to our room, washed up, then climbed into bed. I relaxed against him. Content, I fell asleep in his embrace.

CHAPTER FIFTEEN

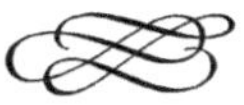

STEFANO

I awoke to light streaming through my bedroom, savoring the feeling of Em sprawled across my chest. For a few moments, everything was right in my world. If only we could have stayed like that, in a bubble where nothing could touch what we had. For years, I'd waited for her, afraid to get too close or let my interest be known. My father was cold, ruthless, and not above using her to coerce me into doing any number of unspeakable acts.

A gust of chilly air swept through the room. It was getting too late into the fall season to sleep with the balcony door cracked open. The night before was likely the last time until spring rolled around. I ran my hand along Em's back, loving her softness. She brought light into my world, something I never thought I would experience.

Em embodied everything sexy, gorgeous, and deadly all in one sensual package. What she experienced years before hadn't broken her in the least. She'd thought it had, in a way, but I hoped our night together laid to rest some of those fears.

She fit into my world seamlessly, as she was both more aware and more vicious than she'd been when she was younger.

For as long as I could remember, I'd been obsessed with her. That wouldn't change—ever. She was mine, and I would kill anyone I deemed a threat to her well-being.

I pressed a kiss to the top of her head, lost in thought about what would need to happen to keep her safe.

She stirred in my arms and lifted her head, blinking sleepily at me.

"Morning."

A soft smile curved her full lips before she kissed me lightly. "Morning."

I tightened my arms around her for a brief squeeze. "You know I'm never letting you go."

Her husky laugh warmed my heart before she fitted herself to me even more, shifting so that she was almost lying across my body. "I'm counting on that. Besides, if you ever tried, you would have a hell of a fight on your hands."

I wound her long hair around my fist and gave it a slight tug. I wanted round two. Every part of me craved her. I wanted to hear the sound of her moan as it slipped past her parted lips, to touch every inch of her and bring her to the edge repeatedly. The joy and pleasure in her eyes was addictive. She needed more of that in her life, and I planned to ensure she had everything she wanted.

"How are you feeling?" I couldn't entirely vanquish the dark memories of seeing her battered and abused, an image that brought me to my knees. I needed reassurance that she was okay, that everything we'd done the night before hadn't brought the nightmares back. I would rather have cut off my right hand than cause her a moment of pain.

"I'm great." She tapped my lips with her index finger. "Stop worrying. There is nothing you do that causes any trigger in me. I trust you completely and am fully present when we're together." She raised to her elbow and brushed her lips against mine in a lingering caress. "Last night was incredible, and I loved every minute of it. But I don't always need gentle, and I don't scare easily, so stop holding back."

"If we keep talking, then yes, I won't hold back. But the second you are uncomfortable or have any mixed feelings, I want to know right away. You're my world, and—"

The shrill ring of my phone brought my thoughts to a halt. Em's eyes turned wary, picking up on my energy. She'd always been good at that. When she shifted off my chest, I eased over to grab my phone from the nightstand.

"I'm going to jump in the shower," she whispered as she scooted to the end of the bed and stood. I hit the answer button but couldn't speak for a moment as I watched her walk into my bathroom, her long hair almost brushing her waist and the perfect curve of her ass and her slender legs that went on for days tantalizing me.

"Stefano," Enzo snapped.

I blinked a few times, clearing my thoughts before I spoke to her brother. I would have to talk to him soon about what had changed between Em and me, but I hoped I could push it off for a little while. "Somebody better have died for you to call at six thirty in the morning."

"Sofia talked with Katya a few minutes ago."

Everything in me hardened as I prepared for more loss. "Is Camila alive?"

"She is. Katya was able to get a burner phone to her and check for bugs where she'll take your call."

I hadn't realized how much the news of my only sibling left being alive would mean to me. "Is she well?"

"Katya told Sofia that she is. The phone will be delivered to Sofia in an hour. We can run it by then. I think she and Lil wanted to come over and hang out with Emiliana some more. I'll let Max know to meet at your place within the hour."

"I'll make sure Em is awake."

"Stay the fuck out of my sister's room," Enzo growled. "I

don't like this situation. She should move in with Sofia and me. I don't know why I ever agreed to this in the first place."

"First of all, you're in the honeymoon phase, and I doubt Em would want to be there while you're fucking like rabbits." I could envision him pacing back and forth and enjoyed his discomfort. "And second, you know why she's here."

"I don't understand it. You're not exactly a warm, fuzzy guy. Why you make my sister calm and feel secure will never make sense to me."

"It's a gift." I couldn't help but chuckle as I threw the covers off and grabbed a pair of sweats to put on as we ended the call. I needed coffee and a lot of it.

I got the machine going then pulled out two mugs and creamer. After mine was ready and I'd taken several fortifying sips, I heard the shower shut off, my cue to get Em's coffee for her.

A few minutes later, she came into the kitchen with her hair still wet, dressed in leggings and an oversized dark-gray sweater. She looked soft and beautiful. I wanted to take her back to bed, and I would have if her brother hadn't been on his way over.

She hopped on to the barstool then wrapped her hands around the mug. "Thank you for this." She took a gulp then moaned. "Best damn coffee ever. I think you could even compete with The Coffee Stop."

I almost choked on my coffee. "Let's not get carried away. I know how serious you and the others are about your complicated coffee drinks."

She set the cup down, her finger tracing the handle before she lifted her serious gaze to mine. "Can I ask about the phone call?"

"It was your brother. He's coming over in less than an hour. Sofia, Max, and Lil should be here too."

"What happened?" Her face drained of color, and I almost kicked myself for not telling her the rest.

"Enzo found out that Camila is alive and well. He's bringing a burner phone for when she'll call."

Em jumped up, rushed around the island, and threw herself into my arms. "That's incredible news!" Then she pulled back, her brows furrowing. "What else aren't you telling me?"

"We still don't know who Frank is working with. I'm delivering the false information about Elena tomorrow morning, and I hope I can learn more then. But it's not looking good. Either way, we'll have to call a commission. The Sicilians will be coming soon."

"No. Nothing good happens with all the bosses in one place." Her fingers dug into my arms. "Will I have to go before them?"

"There is no way we'll let that happen." The thought of Em having to recount what she went through and what Frank said to her made me want to shoot someone. We didn't need her there. It would work out. There were other ways of incriminating him.

And she wasn't wrong—having all the Sicilians and Italian-American bosses under one roof could end up in an explosion of epic proportions should anyone contest what was going to happen.

The more I thought about it, the greater need I felt to bring her fully under my protection, possibly even before the commission. Being Enzo's sister was one thing, but being my wife would provide another level of safety, given what we planned to do in that meeting. Then no one would dare touch her.

I wasn't overjoyed with bringing up a marriage between Em and me to Enzo, but it was necessary. The intercom chimed, and we drew apart to check the monitors to make sure it was the guys. I gave them access to park in the underground garage, and they stepped off the elevator and into my living room minutes later.

By that time, Em was on the other side of the island again, looking the picture of innocence. She jumped up, gave her brother a hug, said hi to Max, and then moved on to the girls, drawing them over to the island for coffee. I snuck one last glance before ushering Enzo and Max into my office, where we would figure out the next steps. I hoped that Em's brother wouldn't shoot me when I brought up my plans for a life with her.

Emiliana

Once Lil, Sofia, and I had coffee, I whipped up some eggs and bacon for us. We took a few minutes to eat, and I contemplated what I could say. I'd promised Stefano I wouldn't share what he told me, but I could poke around the Tony issue. That might help. "I know we sort of ruled Tony out, but what if there's something we're missing?"

"Like what?" Lil tilted her head, her white-blond hair cascading over her shoulder. "All we know so far is that he works a ton of hours at the club and avoids Eva. He hasn't gone anywhere, and we've been tracking him for days."

Sofia stabbed the last of her eggs, popped them into her mouth, then waved her hand in the air. "Look. I'm there with you. We hate Tony. Always have. There might be a shift in his attitude, but who can say for sure? It's not like we hang out with him. He's not a boss, and there's a divide between him and Max."

"I've seen him a few times," Lil added. "He's different. I didn't want to throw a book in his face or shoot him in the leg the last two visits. I don't know… I think managing the clubs is what he needed."

"Purpose." I snagged another piece of bacon. "It makes sense. He was so driven and determined to grab power. We never once considered how Antonio influenced him or that maybe that life wasn't what Tony wanted. I mean, look at Nicole. She went under the knife time and again to please Antonio's exacting trophy wife standards."

"I'm glad he's dead," Lil confessed.

"Aren't we all?" Sofia took the last piece of bacon then got up to make more coffee. "Anyone else?"

Lil and I both declined. I'd already had two cups. Another one so soon would only put me to sleep. Caffeine was weird.

"We could ask Nicole." I still thought she had more information about the connection between her former husband and the Bratva. There was something she wasn't telling us, but I was too shaken the last time we'd talked to push. "I'll meet with her. I think she feels a kinship to me because of Elena and what we both went through."

Sofia dropped her gaze immediately, which was completely unlike her. It wasn't like any of us to keep secrets, and I was positive she had one, but then again, I wasn't telling them everything Stefano had shared with me.

"Call her," Lil prompted then nudged Sofia. "If you want us to, we'll go. Right, Sof?"

"Of course." Sofia blew on her coffee then took a sip.

I paused for another second, waiting to see if she would share. When she didn't, I hit Nicole's contact on my phone. It rang twice before she answered.

"Hi, Nicole."

"Emiliana, it's so good to hear from you."

I leaned back in my chair, genuinely happy to talk to Tony's mom. She didn't miss much and had amassed a great deal of insider information during her marriage to Antonio. She always knew what buttons to push to get the results she wanted. And she'd sided with us girls every chance she'd gotten over the years, even risking her own well-being. All of us liked her.

"It's been a while since we've caught up. I was wondering if you wanted to grab lunch soon?"

"I would love to. How about the day after tomorrow? And maybe you could come here? Max mentioned things were a little precarious, and we should have plenty of guards around. At least for the next couple of days."

Case in point—she was always in the know. "I'd love that." We chatted for a few minutes before hanging up. I met Lil and Sofia's eyes with a nod as the sound of the guys filtered through the living room as they left the office to join us.

They were doing everything they could to hang Frank, but we weren't helpless. I was ready to do my part, too, even if it was only to find out whether or not Tony was guilty.

They stayed for another hour before everyone but Enzo left. Sofia caught a ride to her studio, where my brother had already called in extra guards to wait with her until he showed up. I cleaned a few things up in the kitchen then went out onto the patio to unwind while Enzo talked with Stefano.

I loved it there, with the hypnotic sound of rolling waves, the view, and unlimited access to Stefano. The circumstances might have sucked, but I couldn't have been happier to have that time with him. And honestly, there was no way I would move back home. My home was with him. It was an unspoken agreement between us that would turn into more—my family would never be satisfied with my living with him while in a relationship and not married. Dad had already checked up on me, and after assuring him that I was safe and healthy, he'd wanted to know if Stefano was behaving himself.

I didn't like lying to my dad and would come clean soon. Mom knew. Having her on my side would help when I confessed that Stefano and I were more than friends, that he was the one I wanted to spend the rest of my life with. Mom was thrilled for me. I wasn't sure how dad and Enzo would react, especially since Stefano was Frank Rossi's son, and my dad didn't trust his father in any way.

The sound of Enzo talking with Stefano in the living room faded, and I glanced over my shoulder. Stefano was alone—maybe my brother had left. I slid my legs over the side of the lounge chair then got up. I must have made a noise because he turned as I crossed the threshold from the patio. He stood, rising to his formidable height. Power rippled off of him, and a full-body shiver traveled through me at the promise burning in his dark gaze.

Then he moved toward me, closing the distance in that predatory way he had. No words were spoken. He reached for me, one hand at my hip, the other around the back of my neck, and drew me in. I sighed in pleasure when his lips grazed over mine, and my eyelids closed. The way he made me feel… there wasn't anything better.

My head spun with desire, and tingles spread over my body as the room faded away. I melted against him as he angled my head to deepen the kiss, and beneath my fingers, the muscles in his back shifted and bulged. Electricity sizzled through me as his teasing kiss turned insistent, and I quivered with need.

"What the fuck!"

My brother's bellow tore me from Stefano's embrace. If not for his hand on my hip, I would have stumbled. Fear danced along my spine as Stefano set me to the side right before my brother charged him.

Enzo's fist connected with Stefano's jaw in a sickening crack, his head knocking back. The next second, Enzo went for his gun. Stefano didn't even try to defend himself, but fuck that. I dove at my brother and shoved him before he could point it at Stefano.

"What are you doing?" My hands shook as I pushed at my

brother's chest, trying to hold him back. The sneer on his face and the cold fury in his eyes terrified me. "Stop, Enzo. Please."

"He touched you," he said with a growl, never taking his sight off Stefano, who hadn't moved an inch.

"Yeah." I grabbed his face and forced him to look at me. "I wanted him to. Please, Enzo, don't hurt him. Because if you do, you're hurting me too."

Indecision warred across his taut features. "It's my right, Em. You're my sister. I trusted him to keep you safe, not take advantage of you."

The pain in his gaze shredded me. We had to put the past to rest. I tugged on him to sit with me on the couch. The big-brother protective instinct wasn't unfamiliar to me, but I needed for him to see reason.

"You got one punch in. And by the looks of it"—I glanced over my shoulder at Stefano's swelling jaw, wincing—"you did enough damage." I grabbed his hand, the one not holding the gun. "Think about it, Enz. When you and Stefano told me I was going to move in with him, I didn't put up a fight."

"Of course not. He was supposed to protect you, not maul you."

I rolled my eyes, annoyed with the conversation but determined to break through to him. "I wanted to be here alone with him because I've loved him forever. When we were young? It was always him."

"I'm going to kill him." His body tensed as if to stand. "You're coming home with me."

I clasped onto him harder. "No, I'm not." My voice rang with finality. "After Italy—"

Enzo tore his gaze from Stefano to me, and in one second, his eyes went from enraged to horrified.

"Everything changed. I'm not attracted to anyone. If I tried to date, I know what'll happen because it already has. I'm dead inside. I can't—"

My brother's arms were around me, pulling me in. His hand rubbed my back in soothing circles. "Em—"

"No. It's fine. That part doesn't matter because I don't want to be with anyone else. I love Stefano, and I don't have any of those problems with him. It's as if nothing bad happened to me when I'm with him. We have a connection that cuts through the past. He's my anchor. Please don't hurt him anymore, Enz, because it's the same as hurting me."

Stefano sat in one of the armchairs. "Emiliana is everything to me. I love her."

I could see the anger building in my brother again—*God save me from alpha males. Why couldn't he have brought Sofia with him today? She would have helped so much to distract him.*

"So that's it. I'm with Stefano. Nothing and no one"—I glared at Enzo with my fiercest expression, the one I used before going batshit crazy on him when he did something to piss me off when we were kids—"is going to change my mind or what's going on between us. *Capiche?*"

"Christ, you sound like Sofia." Enzo rubbed a hand over his face.

I couldn't help smirk at how disgruntled he sounded about that. She would have given him hell. All the drama aside, I drew him in for a hug. "Thank you for defending my honor, but he's the one I want. Promise."

"Love you, sis." He squeezed me back then pulled away. "I need to get out of here before I can't stop the urge to hit him again."

Once Enzo was gone, Stefano opened his arms, and I sank into his embrace, taking the strength he offered.

CHAPTER SIXTEEN

STEFANO

After Enzo and Max left, Emiliana and I had spent the day together. Everything had gone smoothly in the meeting with her brother because I hadn't brought up my idea about a quick marriage to his sister. I'd read the room, and it wasn't the time. He was already agitated because Sofia had contact with the Angel of Death again.

It was still early in the morning, and I had a few minutes before I went to my father's when the burner phone I'd left on my desk rang. I didn't recognize the number, but I also didn't expect to. Before it rang again, I snatched it up and pressed the button to accept the call.

"Stefano?"

I would never forget her voice. My hand gripped the phone so tightly that I was afraid I would crack it. "Camila? Are you safe? Do you need extraction?" I wanted her home, but there was no way she would come anywhere near our father.

She laughed, the sound lighter than I remembered—maybe because she was away from how we were raised. "It's only the two of us left, Stefano." Her tone turned somber. "I can't believe

"

it… Mom then Marissa. God, that house is so toxic. I never want to go back there."

I rubbed the bridge of my nose. At least she hadn't been there when Mom jumped. Marissa had. I wondered how much she knew. "How did you find out?" We'd had no contact with her after our father sent her away.

"Vic keeps me informed about our family. He's a good man, Stefano. Things could have worked out so much worse."

"None of us are good, sis. But you're right that things could have been bad. You could have been forced to marry Ivan." I still didn't know how she'd escaped that fate.

"Exactly. Is that why you're calling? To find out about what Yuri has planned?"

"If you know, that would be helpful. What I need to find out is what connection our father has to the Pavlov Bratva and if he's betraying the family in any way."

"I'm sorry." Her voice quieted. "I don't know much about the business. Vic keeps me as far away from them as possible. I'm only around his family when he's by my side. He tries to keep even that to a minimum."

I was grateful. I could have guessed why he felt that way. I would be the same way if I was married to someone I cared about, and it seemed like he did care. The Bratva wasn't like the Italian Mafia—family wasn't everything to them. On top of that, Ivan had been Vic's brother, and I, too, would have done everything within my power to keep my wife away from that psychopath. "Does he talk about business?"

"No. He thinks it's safer for me if he doesn't. And he's probably right."

He was, in a way, but being informed was its own brand of protection. It wasn't the way I wanted things to be with Emiliana. "If you think of anything, Camila, call me. If you need me to get you out of there, I'll be there for you. Our father will never know where I take you."

"Someday, we'll see each other again. I miss you so much, Stefano. Stay strong. I've got to go, but I'll call again soon."

"I love you, sis."

"I love you too."

Not even a second after we hung up, she texted that she would call again soon, the next day if possible. I made a mental note to make sure to keep the burner on me just in case.

For the time being, I put the phone on my desk then went in search of Emiliana to say goodbye. Enzo had given me a thumb drive, which I had in my pocket. I wanted the whole thing finished. We needed my father to make contact with whomever he was working with. Once he did that and made a move on the false trail to the inaccurate location, we would have him, and I would make him pay for everything he'd ever done to my family and Emiliana.

The aroma from the kitchen told me where she was, and I had to pause at the end of the hall where the living room began. I had a clear view of Em while she diced vegetables then threw them in a pan that sizzled with oil. My stomach growled. Too bad there wasn't more time before meeting with my father.

When I moved forward, she stopped what she was doing, put the knife down, and wiped her hands on a nearby towel. "Did you talk to Camila?"

"Yes." I gave her a quick recap of the conversation. "I can't believe she's alive and well. With the luck my siblings and I have, I was sure she would have suffered over the years."

"So she's happy with Vic? I'm guessing he's nothing like his brother."

"I've never met Vic, so I can't say what he's like, but she sounded happy."

"But we're almost back at square one with figuring out who Frank's connection is."

"Unfortunately. And speaking of my father, I've got to go meet him."

Her teeth briefly sank into her bottom lip. "Be careful."

I pressed a kiss to her tempting lips. "Marco is downstairs if you need anything. I'll be back as soon as I can." I hated leaving her, but she was safe here.

After a word with Ren, the captain of the Vitale soldiers, and Marco, I got in my car and sped the half an hour to my father's house. When I arrived, a sense of gloom overcame me when I saw the familiar severe lines of the brick, craftsman-style structure. My stomach tightened and rolled with nausea, rebelling against what the place represented and the years of hell under my father's dispassionate and cruel fists.

Foot soldiers were everywhere on the grounds, watching, armed and ready to defend their boss if an attack occurred. I forced myself to get out of the car, jog up the stairs to the front door, push it open, and go inside. I nodded to a few made men as I moved toward his office. There were fewer made men in the house, and the staff was trained to keep out of sight while maintaining an efficient and spotless manor.

I went down another hallway, and once I was in front of his office, I rapped my knuckles lightly on the door. The gruff "come in" sounded, and I turned the knob and pushed the door open, stepping across the threshold. I shut the door behind me. There was no need for any of his soldiers to hear what I had to say. Nor did I want them to come to his aid if he needed their assistance to restrain me.

My father sat behind his desk, a fat cigar between his fingers. The smoke clung to the furniture and walls with a cloying sweetness. It was nauseating.

Rather than prolong the visit, I pulled the tiny thumb drive from my pocket and tossed it on his desk. "That's what I found on Enzo's server."

An evil gleam sparked in his soulless eyes as he plugged it into his laptop. "Go get her. Bring her here."

"No. That's all I'm doing. You have the information you wanted. Do with it what you will. I'm out of this."

He launched to his feet, his palms flat on his overlarge mahogany desk with the cigar clutched in one hand, the lit end burning the wood's surface.

I unholstered my gun and pointed it at his forehead before he could bellow for the guards. "Let me make this very clear for you. I am not going to go after Elena. If you want her, that's on you. Do not come after me or attempt to do anything foolish. There is nothing you can use against me. You can try, but I promise you, there isn't a single thing you can do to force my hand in this."

There were many things I wanted to say to him, but I didn't. Warning him of what was to come would have been detrimental to catching him in the act of betrayal.

Mocking laughter filled the room as my father pushed away from his desk to stand at his full height of six foot one, an inch shorter than me. "There is always something I can do to bring you back to heel."

"Not this time, old man." I backed out of the room then got the hell out of there. He would issue orders for the men to detain me, but I was done playing games for information. We needed to force him to make a move, and with me out of the picture, that was more likely.

I managed to get to my car and hightail it down the driveway without consequence. Either he was slower than he used to be, which I doubted, or my help didn't hinder the plan he had in place with the Russians and whoever else he had control of in the family.

I'd escalated security where I lived in anticipation of his retaliation and had cameras installed on the nearby buildings, including the roofs and parking entrance and exits. An entire team of my guys monitored for anything suspicious. Given what I'd done, it was possible he would make a move against

Em because he had to know I had her—the only way I would have gone at him like I did was if I thought she was safe. He would count on me underestimating him. I wouldn't. I had endured a lifetime of suffering at his twisted forms of torture.

The trip back to my lakefront home where Emiliana waited took much longer than it should have. Urgency shadowed each step as I strode to the elevator. I needed to see with my eyes that she was alive and safe.

I checked in with Marco and Ren. Nothing had happened so I thanked Marco for coming by then went to the top floor. When the elevator doors slid open and Em greeted me in a red silk negligee, all thoughts fled. She knew what I would need after dealing with my father even without me having to tell her.

She set her glass of wine down, and I closed the distance between us, already unbuttoning my shirt and shrugging out of it. The rest of the room faded away. She shivered as I pulled her into my arms. I planted one hand firmly on her back and buried the other in her hair, cradling her head as my lips slanted over hers in a hungry kiss.

A sexy moan urged me to take more. Sliding my hands down the softness of the silk, I gripped her ass then lifted. She wrapped her legs around me, and I backed her against the wall. I needed her hard and fast. Later, I would take things slow.

She buried her hands in my hair and kissed me back with the same burning urgency. Needing more, I nipped at her lower lip then sucked it to ease the sting. Releasing her lip, I trailed kisses down her neck. She tilted her head to the side to give me greater access. When I found the sensitive spot at the base of her neck and shoulder, I grazed my teeth over the soft skin. She whimpered, arching against me.

My fingers eased along the inside of her thigh, teasing, until I reached the lacy scrap of panties. Her breath came out in little pants, anticipation heightening her awareness. I needed her but managed to hold on to enough control to make sure she was ready for me. I trailed the edge of her the lace then slipped my finger beneath it. I was met by her warm, wet arousal. Groaning, I moved the offensive material to the side then spread her wetness along her seam, circling her clit until her nails dug into my shoulder. I slid one finger in then increased the pressure on the small bundle of nerves until she whimpered, her body convulsing around mine.

Thrusting in and out, I brought her to the edge of release only to pull back, unzip my slacks, and push them down to free myself. I withdrew my fingers and replaced them with the tip of my throbbing cock.

I paused, straining against her but needing her hooded eyes to meet mine. When they did, I asked, "Ready?"

"Yes," she said with a moan, tightening her legs and urging me closer. That was all I needed. In one motion, I pushed inside her. Her back arched, and she cried out, meeting me with each thrust.

Needing more of her, I tore the silk nightgown from her body, baring her breasts. A fine sheen of sweat coated her skin as they bounced before me. My mouth watered. Goddamn, she was beautiful.

Her body fit mine like a glove, squeezing until I swore I would lose my mind. When she gasped, a wave of lust infused my blood. I held still inside her, and her eyes flew open, the protest dying on her lips as I stepped away from the wall so that we were behind the couch. I pulled out, and we both groaned. I managed to tell her to drop her legs. She did, and I spun her around, adding gentle pressure to her back so that she was bent over the back of the furniture.

The lacy panties that I'd shoved to the side needed to come off. I gripped them with both hands and tore them off so that the material wouldn't cut into her skin. With one hand, I grasped her hip and applied a little more pressure to the small of her back. She arched, and I positioned myself at her entrance.

The tip went in, but I remained still, not letting her push back with how I held her. Her long hair fell over one shoulder, so I got a view of the alluring curve of her back.

Resting my hand on the curve of her ass, I spread her enough to accommodate me. Her legs trembled before I thrust deep, seating myself all the way in. There was no stopping this time. One hand slid around her front to find her clit and apply pressure as I pounded into her. Two more thrusts and her body closed in around me, a breathy moan pouring from her mouth as she found her release, and I was helpless but to follow.

I bent around her body while we caught our breath. When my heart rate settled, I withdrew then lifted her into my arms to carry her to the bedroom. Her arms went around my neck, and a sexy smile curved her swollen lips.

"We're not done," I promised, and she laughed, joy sparking in her dark eyes. I planned to worship every inch of her until she was well sated.

CHAPTER SEVENTEEN

EMILIANA

I applied a coat of lipstick stain as Stefano moved behind me and wrapped his arms around my waist.

"You look beautiful." He rested his chin on my head, his eyes heating with desire, something we didn't have time for if I didn't want to be late.

Once finished, I turned in his arms and smiled. "I wish we could stay here today, just you and me."

"You can always cancel with Nicole." His hand applied gentle pressure until I was pressed fully against him, where I could feel his need for me.

Hands flat on his chest, I felt every hard inch of muscle beneath my touch as I slid them up then clasped my hands around his neck. "I can't cancel. But it shouldn't be too long. Do you have anything scheduled after?"

He dipped his head and brushed a teasing kiss across my mouth. I wanted more. My hands tightened on his neck, holding him in place as I parted my lips in invitation. He took the hint and deepened the kiss. I melted into him, addicted in a way I knew wouldn't ever fade.

Tucking a strand of hair behind my ear, he kissed my swollen lips then eased back. Both of us knew the lunch was necessary, even though he'd suggested canceling. He threaded his fingers with mine, and we made our way through the bedroom then the living room until we were at the elevator. When the doors slid open, we stepped inside without a word. I was hyperaware of the weapons strapped to my arms and legs. I was prepared for anything, even with Stefano waiting for me the entire time in the car.

It didn't take long until we were in the Mercedes and headed toward Nicole's house. I was nervous. There was a possibility Tony would be there, and if so, I couldn't ask probing questions about his innocence. If I even hinted at it, Nicole would grasp my train of thought. She was quick that way.

We rode in silence to the Caruso house where Nicole and her son, Tony, lived. The house was enormous, and when we pulled up, my nerves kicked into high gear.

"Hey." Stefano turned my face toward him with two fingers beneath my chin. "What's going on?"

I met his concerned gaze and borrowed some of his strength. "I don't know why I'm anxious. Nicole is great, and she always goes out of her way to make me comfortable. She doesn't even blink if I have my gun out the entire time."

"I get it, but don't let the past define you. You're stronger than that."

He knew. The memories were so close to the surface. The connection to Elena and the pain in Nicole's eyes the last time we were together and talked about her daughter tilted my world on its axis. But he was right. I'd come a long way, and meeting Nicole would be a piece of cake. I gave him a genuine smile then kissed him. "Thanks."

With a sexy-as-hell wink, he pressed one last kiss to my lips then popped the locks on the door and got out. Before he rounded the car, he leaned down and met my gaze. "I'm not going anywhere. I can make calls in the car, right here."

No more stalling.

Stefano opened my door, and I got out of the car, feeling a lot lighter than I had when we arrived. Guards littered the grounds, watching, with guns at the ready. It was my world, and none of it fazed me, not even after the betrayal from within our ranks.

The soldier at the door let me in, saying Nicole was expecting me. I turned toward Stefano with a smile pasted on my lips. He squeezed my hand then let me go.

One of the staff led me through the foyer and into an informal dining room. As I entered the cheery, well-lit space, Nicole stopped midpour and set down a glass of wine.

"Emiliana, you look stunning!" She came around the table and hugged me.

"So do you." And she did. Her makeup was light, and her eyes sparkled with clarity and happiness, something that hadn't been present while her husband was alive.

"It's because I gave up the booze. I mean"—she waved toward the wine—"I'll still drink that but not the hard stuff, and nowhere near what I would put away daily before."

"Things are good, then?" I sat across from her at the table. Her staff swept in and served a meal that smelled heavenly. The atmosphere was relaxed as Nicole thanked them, something I was sure hadn't happened when Antonio ruled the household.

"Yeah, they're pretty great." She twirled her fork in the linguini, lifting it halfway to her mouth, then paused. "Antonio was toxic. With him gone, I'm free, and it's wonderful. I've already redecorated my bedroom and en suite. And I'm renovating the first floor—the reno begins next week. I can't wait. All the bad energy is leaving. Isn't it incredible?"

Antonio had been horrible to her and Max. "It is. How is

Tony adjusting? He was close with his father, wasn't he?" I was shamelessly fishing. She would catch on quickly.

After she finished chewing, she set her fork down and met my gaze. "Tony is dealing with it in his own way. Their relationship was complicated. Antonio didn't bring out the best in my son." A flash of pain flitted across her features as she winced slightly. "But Max has talked to him, and it's helped our relationship immensely."

That was news to me. "He has? What happened?"

Nicole shrugged then took a small sip of wine. "Tony was being, well, his usual obstinate self and mouthed off to me, something Antonio never corrected—he treated me much worse." She dabbed at her mouth, taking a moment. "Max was here that day, something Tony wasn't aware of. I'd told Max he could go through whatever he wanted of Antonio's. When he heard Tony, he took him into the office and shut the door, and they had a lengthy conversation. That's when things began to change. It didn't happen immediately, but there was a definite shift. Tony apologized to me when he came out of the office with Max."

"He's a good guy."

"Max?" Nicole smiled. "He is. I think he was lucky to grow up away from Antonio and have told him that. He's been like a son to me, making sure I'm okay, firing staff, or taking care of guards that don't treat me right." She reached across the table and squeezed my hand. "I love my life and family now."

"I'm happy for you, Nicole. You deserve to be treated with respect." Lil used to talk about Nicole often. My friend had had a soft spot for her when Nicole drank too much. Honestly, I couldn't think of who wouldn't have, given how Antonio controlled and belittled them. And while I knew she was a hard-core opportunist, she was family, and we took care of our own.

"Thanks, darling. But that's not really what you want to know, is it?" She arched one eyebrow.

I couldn't help but grin. She didn't pull any punches, and I loved that about her. "Would Tony betray the family?"

"Oh, doll. If he would, that meant he did so to you and my Elena. While my son has many faults, he isn't evil."

I sank my teeth into my bottom lip, thinking. Something wasn't adding up, but I couldn't put my finger on what.

"The other night, he sat down to talk to me." A soft smile curved her lips upward. "He's loving managing the clubs. Max knew what he was doing with that. Tony is excelling. He's in his element. The success is helping to ease the sting of giving up what he thought was his birthright."

I ate another bite of fettuccini, waiting for her to continue. Whatever it was, I sensed it was big, and I was trying to give her the space to confide in her own way.

"Over the years, he and Eva were an item. It was never out in the open, but they saw each other pretty regularly. Tony's ambitions kept him from letting her in too deep. And I think he cared about her a lot more, but Antonio stopped a deeper relationship from developing. And recently, Tony's been avoiding all contact with her because a few days ago, he saw her with Frank Rossi, and it was not platonic."

"She's sleeping with Frank?" I scrunched my nose. *Ew, Frank is her father's age, and... no. Just no.*

Nicole's lips twitched. "I had the same reaction. But then I thought about it more and realized a few things. Sofia went to Italy with Enzo, to an undisclosed location. Only her parents, brothers, Max, and Lil knew where she was. Not even you knew where she was, and Enzo is your brother. Correct?"

"Yes. But I'm not following where you're going with this." I was, but I couldn't grasp it. *That would mean...*

"Eva knew. Sofia called her, worried about the models and Fashion Week."

"Oh hell no." I jumped to my feet. "Eva's the rat?"

"It seems that way." Nicole set her fork down and threw her napkin on the table, clearly done with the pretense of eating in light of what we were discussing.

I'd lost my appetite too. "Did he tell Max?"

She pursed her lips. "I don't believe so, even though he told me that's what he was going to do."

So many things fell into place. Sofia's location leaked, access to the guard who'd drugged me… Eva had the perfect cover. The night of the attack on Sofia's home, when we were hanging out with her and watching movies, she'd seemed nervous. It was genius how she'd been there during several incidents and had even gotten injured. And she'd been clipped on the head when we were at the restaurant. But her injuries had all been minor and served to solidity her innocence so that none of us would ever question her. She'd always been bitter about how we were royalty and she couldn't shine through when she was with us. I had no idea it went deep enough to make her betray us.

"Why wouldn't Tony tell Max?" I was horrified. The delay could have cost us more than we ever knew.

"Oh, doll." Nicole rounded the table and took my hands in hers. "Tony is a work in process. Going to his brother as his boss, his superior, isn't all that easy. Not yet. All the bad can't be undone in such a short time, but he's working on it. Telling me broke the pattern, and I know he'll continue to get there with Max. He is listening to his big brother. The change in our relationship is proof of that."

I pulled her in for a hug. "I have to go." The words pushed past the tightness in my throat.

"Be careful."

Nicole walked me to the door, and a sense of urgency filled me to run to the car, yank the door open, and scream to Stefano that I knew that the rat in the family wasn't only Frank.

———

Stefano

While Emiliana was having lunch with Nicole, I was able to wrap up three calls I needed to make. But when my burner phone, which I'd brought on the off chance Camila would call, rang, I took pause. She'd mentioned the last time we'd talked that she would try today. I dug it out of my pocket and hit Accept before bringing it to my ear and saying hello.

"Stefano." Her voice sounded breathy and rushed.

"Is something wrong?"

"Hopefully not, but I had to warn you. I had dinner with Vic's parents last night."

I waited for her to continue, a sense of dread hitting me hard at the thought of my sister anywhere near Yuri Pavlov.

"There was a different tension at the table. They haven't forgiven us for Ivan's death. Vic rushed me out of there and increased the number of guards with me and around our property."

"Does he think his family will make an example of you?" I needed to get her out.

"I can't say. Vic doesn't think so, but he isn't willing to take any chances. He's even contemplating bringing me to Italy for a while, but only if he can get away. So far, it's not looking like that'll be a possibility."

"I can get you out."

"And I love you for that. But it's not that bad yet, and Vic will do everything in his power to keep me safe. I love him, Stefano. I'm not leaving. The reason I called wasn't to talk about me. I wanted to warn you about Yuri and his wife, Mischa. She's out for blood and urges Yuri to action."

The Carusos' door flung open, and Emiliana rushed out while Nicole leaned against the doorframe, looking worried.

"I've got to go, Camila. Stay safe and call me if you need

anything at all," I said then shoved the phone in my pocket and opened the door. I rushed around the car, meeting her halfway. My hands gripped her forearms, my gaze darting over her face then to Nicole's and back again. "What happened?"

"I know who else is betraying our family. It's Eva."

CHAPTER EIGHTEEN

STEFANO

We raced home while I called all the bosses: Enzo, Max, and Marco. They would meet us at my place, bringing Sofia and Lil with them. Traffic was heavy, but I wove through it, riding the shoulder when necessary. The problem needed to be contained as soon as possible.

Em vibrated with anger beside me, and I covered her hand. "How are you holding up?"

She turned to me with wide eyes that sparked with deep-seated rage. "Not well. I want to hunt her down and make her pay for every injustice. She was part of our inner circle. Sofia will loser her mind when she finds out that Ivan found her and tortured her because of that bitch. And Lil... my God! We should have taken note and distanced ourselves from her reaction to her cousin. She was never comfortable around her. I can't—"

"Stop. It's not your fault, or Sofia's, or even Lil's for thinking she was one of you. She should have been. Now that we know, we'll do something about it."

"Damn right." Em huffed, crossing her arms over her chest. Her foot tapped a staccato beat.

I swerved as a car tried to block me on the shoulder. Rolling down the window, I stuck out my arm and had my 9mm make the point for me. I aimed low, squeezed the trigger, and buried a bullet in their back bumper. Message received, the car made a fast retreat to their lane. Once the window was back up, I set the gun in the center console.

Em's lips were in a firm line. My fury matched hers. I was just holding it in until I had a target. She was not it, and I kept a tight rein on my anger until we had Eva. I needed the guys there immediately.

The tires squealed as we took the exit, merging off of the highway and speeding toward the underground parking lot. When we got there, three cars were waiting for access. I recognized each one. No one spoke a word as we all parked then filed into the elevator to go upstairs.

Em pushed past everyone and headed for the wine, taking several bottles from the rack and getting to work on opening them. Lil grabbed the glasses while Sofia opened the fridge and riffled around until she pulled out grapes, apples, and a few different kinds of cheese. When Lil noticed what she was doing, she got crackers from the pantry. Em waited until everyone had a glass before taking a hearty sip of wine.

We sat around the living room, and I got down to business. "Emiliana met with Nicole today." My eyes bored into Max. "She had some interesting things to say about what Tony told her." I repeated what Em had told me in the car, and when I was done, Marco and Enzo were both on their feet, pacing, guns out. I got it. Sofia was Enzo's fiancée and Marco's sister. I would have been losing it too. Eva had put her in serious danger.

Max leaned forward, his gaze locked on Em.

Lil looked sick as she whispered, "I'm sorry, Em."

"We don't know whether she was involved in corrupting one of our guards or not." Em shook her head. Her voice was gentle, and I knew she was trying to ease Lil's guilt over what her cousin might have been a part of. "As far as we're aware, the association with Frank is fairly recent. It's something we need to confirm."

"Oh, shit." Sofia's face drained of color. "I called her when we were in Mondello without Enzo knowing. I wanted her to check on the models for me. She could have traced my call. We talked for about ten minutes."

"We kill her," Enzo growled.

Marco had stopped pacing and rested his hands on the back of the couch. "We can't. There's information we need."

I glanced at Em and knew we agreed without having said a word. "And the only way to get it—"

"Is by us"—Em looked at Sofia and Lil—"luring her to wherever we want to hold her for interrogation."

"That would be our place," Max offered. "We have the room."

Lil rolled her eyes. "I guess it's good that I didn't get around to redecorating *that* room yet."

I would have laughed at the way she griped about the room Max had initially held her captive in, but my mood was still too volatile. "The location is settled, then. We need to know the when and how."

"Easy," Sofia said. "I've already talked to her about next year's clothing line and started working on one of the evening gowns I wanted her to wear. I'll tell her we're all trying on the mock-ups that I've made at Lil's. She's an attention whore. She'll take the bait."

"Okay, that takes care of securing Eva." I ran my hands over my face. It was going to be a hell of a plan, one that would line up with the end result the other bosses and I had decided on months ago. "We need to call a commission."

Marco nodded. "I'll do it."

I wasn't boss. It made sense if one of them did. "And the other piece of business."

"Frank," Max supplied. "What are we telling him the commission is about?"

"We need a different rat," Sofia said.

"Tony." Max leaned back on the couch, his arm extending along the back. "We can bring him in only as far as we need to. But this will be a good way of testing his loyalty. We'll give him as much information as necessary, only what we need to use him as bait. It's a new role for him. He's already changed enough to tell Nicole about his suspicions. He knew that if Eva was with Frank, there was something bad going down. Let's give him this chance."

We were doing it. Marco pulled out his phone and made the call to the Sicilians, and Sofia made one of her own to Eva.

I motioned Enzo to step aside with me then led him into the office. This conversation was overdue. The door clicked shut behind him, and I jumped right in.

"You know that by calling a commission, anything can happen—all the bosses together—the Sicilians. Think about it."

Enzo glared from his position across the room, leaning against my desk. I paced, unable to contain the pent-up aggression about what I needed to discuss.

"We know the risks. Why is this suddenly a point of contention?"

"Because it involves your sister," I growled. The thought of leaving her unprotected, even a little, drove me crazy. "She has safety in whose blood flows through her veins. But in the eyes of the Sicilians, her abduction was settled. We eradicated the trafficking ring."

"What's your point?" A muscle pulsed along his jaw.

"That she isn't untouchable." I needed to make it so that she was. Not only that, but she was mine and always had been. "If she's connected to me, and I rise in power, she will be."

"Fuck you." Enzo bolted away from the desk until we were

inches apart. "You're lucky I didn't shoot you when I saw you kissing her. After I explicitly told you not to touch her."

"She's mine. There's no other option. And I didn't do anything until she was ready and initiated herself. I know even more than you do about what she went through after how I found her. I was the one to goddamn pull her out of there!" My hands were curled into fists and shaking. The images were too close, and all I wanted to do was find Emiliana and hold her. "I will never let any harm come to her again. It kills me that she's suffered as much as she has, and I tried to keep her safe for years by staying away. That's not an option any longer. We both know that."

"*Fuck.*" He pivoted away, hands going to his neck as he hung his head. "I hate the thought of it."

Seconds passed in silence while I waited for what he would do. Either turn around and hit me again or see reason in this fucked-up situation.

"This will have to be quick." Enzo turned and glared. "I don't like it. All I want is for my sister's happiness and safety. And if you upset her, even a little, I'll come for you."

"I wouldn't expect anything less." If it were Marissa, I wouldn't have let her stop me from shooting him for touching her. The only reason Emiliana was able to was because of her past. She'd been through too much for Enzo not to take into account any protest she had. The situation was different.

"We'll need to do this quickly. This Saturday."

"That's tomorrow." Enzo's mouth was in a thin line.

"It is. We do this with you, Marco, and Max present. That'll have to be enough because there is no way we'll include my father. And once I'm boss, it won't matter anyway."

"I'll take care of the donation to the church and the priest. We do this early, like Max and Lil's ceremony before the one for show. At the ass crack of dawn."

"She'll need a dress."

"I'll see what Sofia can come up with. She may have something designed already that she can alter for Em."

"I need to go to the jewelers." I glanced at my watch. It didn't matter what time it was. They'd close the store for me or even come in after hours. I had to make one phone call, and it would be done. Since Enzo agreed, I wanted to get moving on the ring.

"I'll stay with my sister. Go." He went to the door and yanked it open.

I barely stopped the grin from curving my mouth. I could make this so much worse for him, and I was tempted to, but I needed to make some phone calls.

Em was on the couch when we came out of the office, with a glass of wine in hand and flipping through a magazine. Something amazing was simmering in a pot on the stove, and my stomach growled as if on cue. Enzo laughed as he went into the kitchen.

I reached for her hand, and she set the magazine aside as I drew her to her feet. God, she was so beautiful. Her dark hair curtained her stunning face. Plump lips tempted me. Since her brother had already punched me over kissing her and agreed to my marrying her, I gave in.

My hand threaded through her silky hair as I bent and brushed my lips across her soft ones, begging entry. She melted against me, and I deepened the kiss, losing myself in the decadence of her. Heat built between us, and if it weren't for Enzo's loud clearing of his throat, I would have taken things further.

Breaking the kiss with reluctance, I pulled away. "I have to run out but will be back in a couple of hours. Enzo is staying."

"Okay." Her fingers tightened on my biceps for a half second before she released me. "Be safe."

I understood the sentiment. I didn't want to leave her either. The worry reflecting back at me made me want to hurry back to her even more. I pressed a kiss to her forehead then went to the door.

"Too bad there won't be any food left when you get back." Enzo's parting comment made me laugh, especially when Em's temper flared, and I knew he was precariously close to not getting anything to eat now.

The elevator doors closed, the ride short, then I was in my car, the jeweler already on the line. Next, I called Max and talked to him and Lil. She would handle the flowers. The priest, and paperwork, were the final loose ends, but I wasn't worried. I would stop by after I had the ring. I wanted the best for Emilana. We just had to do this fast and keep it from my father and everyone else.

Emiliana

After convening at Stefano's lakefront home, Sofia and I had gone with Lil to her and Max's place. It wasn't far from Stefano's and had the convenience of the secure room where we could interrogate Eva.

I twirled my wineglass by the stem, doing my best to keep the vortex of emotions locked away. We'd decided to invite Eva over that evening after the meeting wrapped up. There was no call to wait and every reason to act. The longer she was left to her own devices, the more damage she could inflict on us.

Frank was another story altogether. I wasn't going to take him on. That was all on Stefano. But we would handle Eva, and by the steely determination reflected at me in Sofia and Lil's eyes, they were feeling everything I was, maybe more.

Sofia had called Eva, and she was en route to Lil's place, where we gathered. The guys weren't there, but they were nearby and would descend not long after she arrived. We wanted more time and hoped they would back the hell off and let us do our thing.

We had zip ties and rope ready. A recorder was already set up in the room and on. We wanted undeniable proof in the form of her confession. It wasn't going to be a pleasant experience. She was one of ours. But what she had done without regard to who was killed, *or how*, shattered the friendship or sentimentality we used to share. Just closing my eyes and remembering Sofia's torture at Ivan's hand and my stint with the human trafficking ring brought a surge of rage from within me. There would be no leniency where Eva was concerned. "Do either of you want wine? We should look normal for when she walks in, at least."

"Oh, right. Yes," Sofia said. "And she should be here any minute now."

Lil's phone chimed. "That's her. I'm letting her in." She granted Eva entrance to the underground parking garage then the elevator.

We waited with bloodthirsty anticipation. The bitch was going down.

When the elevator dinged, Eva stepped into the living room in a flurry of motion. She flicked a lock of her thick, dark-brown hair over her shoulder, and her red lips curved into a wide smile. "I'm here!" On her way to where we waited at the island, she tossed her purse on the couch in reckless abandon—mistake number two. The first one was trusting us in the first place, given what she'd done.

The wine was next to me on the island, and my friends were each seated on a bar stool with a glass in hand. Lil lifted hers in a salute then took a sip. I poured Eva a glass as she neared. When she went to reach for it, I whipped out my gun and pointed it at her chest.

"What? Was this yours?" Eva raised her eyebrows, and a touch of wariness infused her features. "Or are you mad I didn't bring more wine?"

Lil and Sofia drew their guns and aimed them at her as well.

"Let's go," Lil directed, tilting her head toward the hallway that led to the spare room where Max had locked her up for a night when he was trying to save her.

Eva backed toward the elevator. Sofia moved behind her and pushed the barrel of her Glock into Eva's back. "Move. This is us being nice. We could knock you out and drag you where we want you."

"I have no idea what this is about. Who shit in your corn-flakes this morning and poisoned your mind against me?"

"That would be you," Lil said.

"I'm gonna go. You're all acting crazy." She took a step in the wrong direction.

I'd had enough and rushed her. I slammed the butt of my Glock into her temple, and she crumbled to the ground, uncon-scious. Lil and Sofia didn't say a word, just grabbed her arms and legs then dragged her into the secure room. Once inside, I patted her down and removed the sheathed knives and a small gun. Then we got her into the chair and zip-tied her arms and legs to it. We wrapped the rope around her legs and through the chair, continuing to hold her middle to monitor for any sort of movement.

"Do you have any smelling salts?" I asked Lil, wanting Eva awake and answering questions before the guys came up.

"Yeah. I'll be right back."

Sofia met my gaze as Lil went to get the salts. "I'm texting the guys that she's secured but to stay the hell out of the room for now. They can listen from the hall. This is our right."

I nodded, the need for vengeance strong. "Agree. She may have betrayed the family, but we let her in to our circle, and for that, she answers to us."

Lil returned. Eva's head hung forward, so Lil grabbed the back of Eva's hair and pulled until her face angled toward the ceiling. Sofia set the smelling salts on her upper lip and let them rest there to do their job.

It took a few seconds until Eva's eyelids raised, and she made a face from the smell. Lil removed the salts, and we gave her a little more time to acclimate back to consciousness. When she did, it was with a roar.

"What the fuck is this all about?" Her eyes flashed with fury, and she strained against the bindings.

My fist connected with her face. The satisfying crunch of her nose did little to quell my outrage at what she'd allegedly done, but it did shut her up, and I felt marginally better. "You know what this is. Start talking about your connection with Frank."

Blood trickled down her face, and she sneered at the three of us. "It's sex, that's all. I'm tired of Tony's rejection. Nothing I do makes him choose me."

Lil snorted. "You're telling us you're attracted to Frank? Nope. Not buying that. Try again."

Eva rolled her eyes then winced, probably from how they were swelling underneath her broken nose. "I'm attracted to Frank's power and money, not anything else."

"Maybe." Sofia stepped up. "But you're sneaking around. And somehow, Ivan found out where I was staying in Italy. Want to tell me about that?"

"A lot of people knew where you were." Eva sneered. "Why don't you question them?"

Sofia snorted. "My parents? My brothers? Or maybe Max and Lil. Is that what you're getting at?"

"Lil would be top on my list." Eva glared at her with malicious intent.

"Try again." Lil moved forward, delivering another punch to Eva's face. Blood spurted from her nose and split lip. "Huh, I like your face better like that."

Eva sneered. "You've never liked me."

"You're not wrong." Lil got into her space, leaning down so that they were at eye level, only inches apart. "I should have listened to my instincts where you were concerned. I won't make that mistake again. I don't have to. You don't have long to live."

The ding from the elevator sounded, and Lil moved back to shut the door so the guys wouldn't come right in. We needed more time.

I unsheathed one of my knives then buried it in Eva's left thigh. She screamed in pain and rage. Her nostrils flared, spraying droplets of blood onto her clothes. I yanked the blade out then sank it into her arm, where I left it for the time being. "Who did you tell about Sofia? Frank or Ivan?"

A deranged laugh left Eva's lips. "I'm not telling you anything."

I shared a look with my friends. It was time to get inventive. "Waterboarding?" It was less bloody than tearing her fingernails off or making small cuts all over her body—they hurt like a bitch but weren't fatal.

Lil left to get a bucket we could fill with water. It took her a few minutes before she returned, probably because the guys were giving her a hard time and wanted to be in on the interrogation. We would need a few hours, but we would get what we were after in the end.

After Lil returned, we dragged Eva into the bathroom, still tied to the chair. Sofia cut the ties for Eva's hands then tipped her chair back so she lay on the ground, legs up and over her heart from where her ankles were still tied. Sofia yanked her hands over her head, applying weight so she couldn't move. Lil wet a washcloth and placed it over Eva's face so that the water we poured would go into her mouth and nose but couldn't be expelled.

Then it was my turn. I filled the bucket a quarter of the way full then stood over Eva while Lil pressed on her TMJ joint, located on the side of her head and in front of her ear. With her jaw open, I poured the water into her mouth in a steady stream.

She thrashed and gagged as much as her limited movements allowed. When the bucket was empty, Sofia and Lil jerked the chair upright. The washcloth fell off her face while she coughed, vomited water, and gasped for air.

We gave her a moment, asking who she was ratting us out to. When she refused, we waterboarded her repeatedly then threatened electrocution. Sofia went into detail about what it would feel like as she was recently subjected to it, courtesy of Ivan.

We dragged her back into the bedroom, where we broke two of her fingers and a rib and delivered several blows to her body that left ugly bruises that were already forming. She wasn't in the best shape. It was wearing her down, and we were closer to getting the answers we needed. Eva was driven, not stupid. Things would get a lot worse if she didn't give us something. Sofia and Lil had taken turns questioning her.

For my turn, I brought out the cigar cutter. "Look familiar? Frank gave it to me."

"He didn't." Eva's voice was raspy, weak, and riddled with pain.

"How do you think we figured out it was you? He told us that you're the rat we've been searching for."

I didn't even have to look to know that Sofia and Lil went along with me as if what I said was fact. Eva's eyes glazed with a hollowness we hadn't achieved by working her over.

"Let's try this again." I was at eye level with her while she was tied to the chair, giving her a hard gaze as I slipped the cigar cutter over her pinky finger. "What was your connection to Ivan?"

"He approached me in college. Thought we could help each other out."

Dread seeped into me because of the timing. Theirs was a long relationship, and nothing good could have come from it.

"He was searching for Elena, but we'd already heard of her death. I relayed the details, something he left to investigate."

"What did you want in return for that?" There was no way she wouldn't broker a favor. It was in her nature.

A sigh slipped past her lips, and her lids lowered over her eyes. "Marissa."

Holy shit. My gaze jerked to Sofia then to Lil. Before Eva could see my shock, I schooled my features and returned my focus to her. Lil moved back to the opposite end of the room, taking a minute to compose herself. Sofia vibrated with barely contained fury and anguish. She was a volcano waiting to erupt on Eva. I needed Sofia to hold it together.

"She was your friend. You and Marissa were close. Why would you want to hurt her?"

Sofia took a step forward, and my gaze shot to her, ordering her with my eyes to wait. It wasn't yet time to do more.

"Tony was mine. We'd been seeing each other for years. Then Antonio got in his head, telling him they needed more power, more connections, and that he was to marry Marissa to gain a tighter alliance with the Rossi family because he wasn't sure Frank would let Stefano live anyway, and Tony could end up leading that arm of the family."

It went a lot further back than we'd thought. My gut churned, and my throat tightened. I needed just a little more out of her before we turned her over to the guys. "So you had Ivan kill her?"

Eva nodded once. I waited, needing to hear the words. "Eva."

"Yes."

A mere whisper, but it was enough. I removed the cigar cutter and handed it to Sofia.

"Marissa's murder was to win Tony back to your side. But it didn't work, and you grew bitter," Sofia said as she stepped up and I moved back closer to where Lil stood with horror pulling her features taut. "Didn't you?"

Eva's eyes filled with hatred, and her lips pulled back in a sneer. "He never wanted me, not really. So I decided to take what he did want."

"What was that?" Sofia pushed.

"The Rossi family."

I left Lil's side and moved so that I had a clear view of Eva's face. I needed to hear what other hellish things she'd done, especially if it had anything to do with Stefano.

Sofia continued to question her. "And you went straight to Frank because he's boss, not Stefano."

"Why go to his son? It could take years, decades, until Frank relinquished the position. And we all know he wouldn't unless it happened through his death."

"And that's where your allegiance to Frank began. You would do whatever he needed doing against the family, and he promised you marriage?"

"He wanted Emiliana out of the way. She was a distraction to Stefano, and he wanted complete control over his son's life. I didn't know any details. All I was supposed to do was find a guard that could be bribed. He took care of the rest."

I was done. Black spots converged, blurring my vision, and I turned away, my palm flat on the wall in an attempt to ground myself. She'd just confirmed that she was the reason the guard had betrayed me. Frank was the one who'd sold me out to the human traffickers.

I let myself out of the room and walked straight into Stefano's waiting arms on the other side of the door. The soft click told me he'd closed it again, cutting off any view Eva had of us.

The guys had hunted and dealt with the guard who'd betrayed me. Ivan's death was another piece of the puzzle, but we'd never connected anyone else to the leak, thinking the guard had acted on his own with influence from an outside source—maybe the Russians, possibly the cartel. We'd kept watch over their actions but hadn't located the rat.

Now, we had, and there were two of them.

The soothing feeling of his hand rubbing circles on my back helped to calm my frantic pulse as I rested my cheek against his solid chest. I relayed everything that we'd done in halting words, still shocked by the horror of Eva's betrayal. With each revelation, Stefano's body tensed, rage vibrating off him.

"You're right to use Tony as bait to lure Frank without suspicion to the meeting." I needed for it to be over, and I never wanted Frank to have any hold over Stefano again.

CHAPTER NINETEEN

EMILIANA

We'd arrived home from Max and Lil's only moments before. It was late, and we were both tired. The sun had sunk below the horizon, taking with it the fiery oranges and reds that had painted the water in brilliant hues. Stefano had calls to make, men to check in with who were guarding us, or whatever else was on his lengthy list to do. I'd decided to take a shower and, after towel drying my hair and leaving it to air-dry, I went to the living room to find the lights off and what looked like a hundred candles on every surface ablaze. If it hadn't been for the modern furnishings, I could have pictured another time.

Then my gaze landed on Stefano, who emerged from the shadows. The soft light flickered, dancing over his beautiful features and angular planes, highlighting the predatory way he moved. Captivated, I couldn't tear my gaze from him.

My voice was a whisper in the silence, "What's going on?"

I tilted my head back as he stopped before me, all leashed strength and power. Then he cupped my face, his thumb rubbing back and forth over my lower lip, drawing me into the spell where only the two of us existed. My skin buzzed with sizzles of electricity beneath his touch, and my mind stilled as if waiting on a precipice for what he would say. The space around us pulsed with love, desire, and a timelessness that brought a fine sheen of tears to my eyes. I could drown in the way he looked at me, as if I was precious, cherished, the very air he needed to breathe. We existed in the moment.

Then he bowed his head until his lips brushed over mine in a dizzying caress. He teased and drew me close. In his arms, I was safe, protected, and loved. With him, I would never want for anything.

When he straightened, I sighed, my hands tight around his shoulders, clinging to him. He tucked a lock of damp hair behind my ear, and I shivered in the wake of his touch.

"I've walked alone in darkness for most of my life." His deep, gruff voice teased my ears with the hypnotic vibrations that traveled from his chest to mine. "Existing that way, except for those rare moments of sunshine when you graced me with your presence. The stolen kisses, the way your touch healed the deepest wounds that lived where no one ever saw. But you did." He traced the pad of his finger across my lower lip again. "In those fleeting moments, you saved me. You gave me a reason to live, to want, to persevere."

I rose on my toes and brushed my lips across his, pulling away before we took things further. "If I saved you when we were younger, you were the lifeline when I was drowning. When despair threatened to suffocate me all those hours— weeks—in hell, all I had to do was draw strength from my memories of you. There was no doubt in my mind you would come for me if I weren't able to free myself. You will always come for me." I smiled because there was no sadness in what we were saying. There was only hope. "But we're no longer there. We're in the light, together, as much as the Mafia allows."

His hands moved to my hips, holding me close. "And that's what I want. For us to be together. For the world to know that no one can ever take you from me again. I want to spend the rest of my life with you by my side. Hearing your laughter, seeing your beautiful smile, sharing every day with you. Will you be my wife, Emiliana?"

"Yes." I grinned. "Even though in my heart, I already am."

"You've always been mine."

Then he kissed me. And when he lifted me into his arms and carried me into our bedroom, I knew he would make my every fantasy come true.

—————

Stefano woke me before the sun rose with the rich aroma of coffee. He coaxed me out of bed, into the shower and, after I dressed, to his waiting car. Once the caffeine was pumping through my system, I tried to pry out of him where we were going, but he only grinned. An expectant and almost nervous energy buzzed through the car. It wasn't until we arrived at the cathedral with its gothic architecture and stained glass windows that our destination was revealed. It was where many of the Cosa Nostra's weddings were held.

Excitement pinged through me as he took my hand in his then led me inside. A small nudge in the direction of where I'd waited for Lil not too long ago, and I laughingly brushed a kiss over his sinful lips before heading to where I knew my friends would be waiting.

I could hear the music thumping before I even opened the door. Stefano grinned, pressed a quick kiss to my lips, then murmured that he'd see me in half an hour. My hand hovered over the doorknob as I watched him walk away, all six-foot-three inches of imposing muscle and deadly power. I swore my heart tripled in pace. I couldn't believe I was marrying him in thirty minutes.

The smile on my face was wide as I twisted the handle,

already knowing what to expect when the door swung open. The minute Lil and Sofia spotted me, they rushed forward with ear-piercing shrieks. Joy filled me, and I threw my head back and laughed as I was caught up in their hugs.

When they released me, Lil grabbed an already poured mimosa and handed one to me and one to Sofia before she picked hers up and lifted it in a toast. "To secret weddings."

Both Sofia and I chuckled. Lil and Max got married in a very similar situation. "To marrying our soul mates." The glasses clinked as we tapped them lightly together.

"When did he propose?" Sofia asked, brushing her long, wavy hair over her shoulder. "Last night?"

"Yep." I laughed at her eye roll. I knew what she was thinking.

"I've been engaged far longer, and still, I'm the last to get married. Enzo and I are going to have a little chat after you say 'I do.'"

"I would join you in that just to watch Enzo try to dig his way out of that one," I teased. Sofia huffed, and I couldn't help but feel a little bad, even though she was kidding. I got serious, dropping all levity from my voice. "You know he loves you and has forever."

"Yeah"—she flashed a dreamy smile—"I know it. But it's fun to give him a hard time."

"Hey." Lil clapped her hands. "We have twenty minutes. Sit your ass down, Em. We've got hair and makeup to do, and Sofia has a surprise."

My heart flipped, but I didn't dare hope she had a dress for me. There was no time, and Stefano didn't stipulate what I needed to wear. I'd thrown on a pair of pants and a sweater. It wouldn't have been my first choice had I known where we were going, obviously, but I would make it work. Lil tugged on my hair, separating it in clumps as she curled each section.

I sipped on my mimosa until Sofia reappeared, a garment

bag in hand. I sucked in a breath, the vodka-spiked orange juice went down the wrong pipe, and I had a coughing fit.

"No more for you." Lil moved my glass out of reach but winked at my reflection in the mirror. She released my hair from the iron so that I could turn and face Sofia.

"What did you do?" There was no way she'd had time to make anything, and I worried that what she held in her hands was the dress she'd been designing for her wedding. "Please tell me you didn't bring me your dress, because I won't wear it. That's not fair to you."

Sofia hung the bag on the back of the bathroom door then spun around, hands on hips. She was the smallest of all of us, but I'd always felt she had the most outgoing personality. Her presence made her seem tall and added vibrance to any room.

"No and no. This is a new design I was toying around with for next year's Fashion Week. Luckily, it was one of the sketches I'd already begun work on. I just had to do a few alterations last night after Enzo—that's right, he told me, not you—about the wedding."

Heat crawled up my neck and settled in my cheeks. "We were busy last night."

Lil snorted, choking on her drink. I plucked it from her fingers then patted her back.

"Guess we're both cut off." She shook her head then rolled her eyes. I felt bad about not reaching out to them. I would have if Stefano hadn't distracted me so well and for so many times last night. "I'm sorry. I planned on calling first thing this morning, but he got me up early—"

"At the ass crack of dawn." Sofia huffed.

"And I barely had time to get dressed before he had me out the door and on our way to the church."

"We get it, Em." Lil finished the last few sections of my hair, and it fell in loose beachy waves. "We're just glad to be here and to share in your day. It's about time you and Stefano got together."

"We've only got a few minutes. Ready to see the dress?" Sofia asked. "We're doing a black-and-white theme. Does that work for you? It was the easiest for finding two similar dresses for us."

"Yep, it totally works."

Lil went to another garment bag and withdrew two black sheath dresses. Classic. I hoped we would have pictures. Then Sofia unzipped the bag and pulled out a beautiful chiffon gown in white with a fitted lace bodice, plunging sweetheart neckline, and dramatically flared skirt. My mouth worked, but no sound came out. Speechless, I ran my fingers over the delicate fabric. "It's stunning, Sofia."

"Not nearly as gorgeous as you." Sofia's eyes teared before she blinked the moisture away. "Get out of that dress so I can help you with this one."

After I stripped down to my bra and panties, I stepped into the dress and let Sofia and Lil fuss over me. We had seconds before it was time to go out there, and my emotions were all over the place. I couldn't have been happier to have my two best friends by my side, even when Lil slipped an extra knife down my cleavage—just in case. I didn't think we'd have any trouble. Stefano had promised that the only people that knew about what we were doing were the ones here. All the bosses but Frank Rossi were there: Marco, Max, and Enzo.

There was every reason to make sure he wasn't there, and I was all for it. Then it was time, and the girls flanked me as we walked down the hall to enter the vestibule. I sucked in a breath as the doors opened, and I caught a glimpse of Stefano flanking the altar, waiting for me. As at Lil's secret wedding, there were hundreds of candles in all shapes and sizes, creating a beautiful and timeless atmosphere. I couldn't help but think it was the continuation of a tradition for us. Sofia would have to get married to the same, whether she had a second public wedding later or not. This was an experience we all needed to have.

I glided down the aisle with my hand tucked into the crook of my brother's arm, my eyes locked on Stefano's. The room faded so that he was all I could see. After Enzo handed me off and I stood before him, every inch of my body swooned. He had the devastating good looks that stopped you in your tracks. Danger radiated from him, the kind that sunk into your bones. His tailored suit fit his sinfully powerful body to perfection. Despite the outward appearance, he was beautiful on the inside as well, with his fearless protection. My body trembled with how in love I was with him.

Our gazes met, and I saw the world that he would give me in his eyes. Everything else faded. The priest performed the wedding, but I barely heard a word of it, only responding when it was my turn to do so. Stefano slipped a round eight-carat diamond ring in a pave setting and matching band on my finger. Then we were pronounced husband and wife. His lips were on mine, and I melted into him, overjoyed that he was my husband.

When we broke apart, I swore my brother growled. I heard a smack and whoosh of air. I didn't have to turn to know Sofia had smacked him in the stomach. Our marriage documents were signed and put into Stefano's inside suit jacket. I knew a large donation had been made to the cathedral, and after the blessing, we were off. There was no reason to stay any longer than necessary. Stefano didn't want word to get back to his father. Not yet anyway.

I hugged Lil and Sofia before the guys. Then we were in the car and racing back to our lake house. So weird—it was our home. I grinned at Stefano as the thought hit me. His hand rested on my thigh, and for the first time in years, I was utterly content.

CHAPTER TWENTY

STEFANO

Two days had passed since we'd learned what Eva had done. Marco, Max, Enzo, and I had each taken a turn talking to her, but the girls had done the hard work and gotten what we needed. Max had informed Frank about the commission as I was technically his second and wouldn't have known of the meeting before him, at least in the scenario worked out between the four of us.

It was early morning, and Emiliana and I were in our lakefront home, not even out of bed yet. She was tucked against my side, resting her head on my arm, and our legs tangled together. Coffee was a must, given how little sleep we'd gotten the night before. I couldn't stop touching her, needing to reassure myself that she was there, that Frank hadn't stolen her from my bed and killed or tortured her while I slept unknowingly. The fear was unwarranted—the building was secure—but I couldn't shake it. He'd already taken her from me once.

There was only one way that nightmare would ease its grip, and that was if Frank was dead. I glanced at the clock, counting the hours until showtime.

The Sicilians would arrive that evening, going directly to the warehouse from the airport. Max and Lil had kept Eva contained and alive at their lakefront home. We would get there before well before they did with Eva and Tony. There could be no leaks of her presence, and Max had Vitale, Caruso, and La Rosa soldiers stationed around the premises to ensure Frank didn't station his men there as well.

But for the next few hours, it was all about Emiliana—*my wife*. I would spend the rest of my life making her happy, not only because I wanted to with every fiber of my being, but also because of my father's betrayal and the way his evil had touched her life.

Em stirred in my arms, and I turned to her as she opened her eyelids to half-mast. She was soft and relaxed, and I wanted her all over again. It was a need that would never go away.

"Morning." I brushed a kiss across her lips.

"Mm." She stretched languidly, a small smile curving her mouth. "Morning."

I tucked a piece of her hair behind her ear, following the curve of her check, then ran my fingers beneath her chin, urging her to meet my kiss. She did. Eagerly. I traced the seam of her lips, begging entry. When she parted them, I deepened the kiss, changing the pressure and tempo the more I explored her softness, her taste. I would never get enough of her.

A moan slipped from her parted lips, and I swallowed the sound then broke the kiss, tugging on the hair at her nape until she gave me access to her neck. I trailed kisses from her mouth to that sensitive spot on her neck, grazed it with my teeth, then gently bit down. Her nails dug into my shoulders, and she gasped.

The clothes between us had to go. I slipped my hand beneath her sleep tank, pushing it up then over her head until her breasts were bare. I cupped one while lavishing attention to the other. Her body was soft against my hardness, her skin silky smooth compared to mine. Everything about her tasted of decadence.

Needing to sink into her heat, I pushed her panties down, and she kicked them off. My fingers grazed her slit, and she moaned my name as she shoved the covers aside. I flipped her on top of me. I wanted her to have control.

With her palms flat on my chest, her hair curtained around her face as she rubbed herself over my cock. So fucking gorgeous. I gripped her hips, increasing the friction, and her tongue darted out, running along her plump bottom lip. She adjusted me so that the tip of my cock was at her entrance. When her lips curved into a devilish grin, I laughed, feeling a foreign lightness pierce my heart. She was my light, my salvation.

I sat up so I could kiss her, my hands guiding her hips. When she sank down, I clenched my teeth at the feeling of her surrounding me. She felt so right. I kissed her as we moved together, our bodies heated and hypersensitive. She shifted her hips, increasing speed and bringing both of us closer. My fingers found her clit and rubbed until she cried out, her body clenching mine and hurtling me over the edge with her.

Our bodies were slick with sweat, and she laughed, her forehead resting against mine. Neither of us moved. I wanted to savor the moment a little longer. As soon as we got up, our day would begin. And while I looked forward to the commission later that night, I knew there was always room for errors, sometimes fatal, and I planned to spend every moment I could with the woman I loved.

Her fingers traced lazy circles over my abs. "How long until you have to leave?"

I pulled her close, knowing there wasn't as much time as I would have liked. "In a couple of hours."

"Let's go to the beach and just walk around a little." She tilted her head so that our gazes met.

"We're too close to the meeting, and walking along the beach could cause a risk. Let's play it safe a little while longer. Besides" —I couldn't stop the grin even if I tried—"I got you something. Get some workout clothes on. We're going in the basement."

"Oh—" She laughed. "I like where this is going."

Once we were dressed and she'd braided her hair, we went to the floor beneath the garage where her training gym was set up. For the small amount of time she'd lived with me, the studio had already seen a lot of use. It was about to get more.

I'd left the new weapons I'd bought for her there, knowing I would give them to her today. My hand rested on her hip as we walked to where the sleek, old-world karambit knives were displayed. The blades were curved, the handles ergonomic. They were formidable weapons worthy of the fighting style Emiliana exhibited.

We stood before them, and Em lifted a hand, tracing a finger along one handle before she plucked it from the display stand. "They're gorgeous."

I grinned then went to the side panel that housed the rubber knives. I'd purchased two sets in the same shape as the karambit knives she held so that we could spar with them. Eventually, she would demand we use real ones, but we were going to spar with the rubber version for now.

Besides, the practice ones held a certain level of danger. They could still cause injuries and cuts. When she saw what I had, she returned the new weapons to their stand and took the set I offered.

"I thought we could spar. We have time before I leave."

Laughter spilled from her lips, and she flipped her long braid over her shoulder. "I would love that."

While Em turned on music, I grabbed the second pair of curved rubber knives. Before I'd fully straightened, I caught movement from the corner of my eye and lifted my arm to block her first strike. I stepped into the strike, pushing her knife-wielding hand to the side. She moved into my body, her other knife on the path to sink into my engaged arm's bicep. Releasing the pressure to her first attacking strike, I clamped onto her wrist as she aimed for my bicep. Her freed arm came under the bridge of our arms and struck my stomach.

She was a master at the path of least resistance with her fighting style, which served her well against bigger and stronger opponents.

Over and over, we went at it. She would go inside the arc, and then I would. Over the arc, twisting my arm, then bending her elbow and sinking the pseudo blade into my ribs. She attacked. I grabbed her wrist, twisting until she went to a knee. I released her quickly then sank my blade between her shoulder and neck.

Again, we met in a flurry of movement. I grabbed her arm, stopping her blade from slicing me. She twisted my wrist, applying pressure to my thumb until it would break if I didn't move with her. Her knife tagged me. The tallies were adding up. She was ahead. But my combat skills exceeded hers. We both had work to do, and I looked forward to every minute of it —together.

We sparred for an hour. Sweat slicked our bodies, and with each brush of hers against mine, I became more aware of her until I couldn't resist her any longer and dropped my knives on the mat. One step closed the distance between us. My hands framed her face, then my lips crashed down on hers. I vaguely registered the thud of her rubber knives before she opened for me, her tongue tangling with mine.

I wanted to sink into her heat more than anything, but our time was limited. I couldn't help myself from kissing her, and I used every minute we had to taste and tease her. She melted against me, her fingers splaying in my hair, and as I lifted her in my arms, her legs automatically wrapped around my waist.

I carried her to the elevator. When the doors slid open, I

stepped inside, our lips never parting. It wasn't long until we were on the top floor and then in our bathroom. Reluctantly, I broke the kiss, but only to peel her clothes from her body. I had ten minutes until I had to go to the meeting. She helped by tugging at mine until we were both naked and underneath the rainfall showerhead. I planned to make the most of every second we had before leaving by doing what I loved best.

This is it. My body hummed in anticipation for what was to come. Frank had wanted me to arrive with him, and I had little choice but to do as he commanded, although it would be the last time.

I rode in the back seat of Frank's car. His driver pulled up to the warehouse as several identical black cars slid into parking spots.

Enzo, Marco, and Max were already there. Tony was inside and tied to a chair, but the bonds were loose. We'd gagged him, so if Frank or one of the Sicilians tried to interrogate him, he had a pass. His role would be short-lived. The real reason for the meeting had to happen soon after we began.

The Sicilians were there. Men my father's age and older who wore black suits, and one with a fedora, got out of cars. They grunted in greeting, and we piled into the building with a sense of wariness making our steps heavy. But beneath the defensiveness was a palpable rage for what was to come. We had discovered a rat and called in all the heads of the family to witness the elimination.

Max and Enzo stood on either side of Tony. The conversation broke out immediately when the old guys saw who it was. I wanted to punch Frank's smug expression off him. But I couldn't do a thing yet.

Vincenzo Brambilla, the oldest of the Sicilians and grandfather to Liliana, regarded the Chicago bosses curiously. Either he was on to us, or Max had told him what was about to happen.

As expected, Frank took it upon himself to start the meeting. We were ready for that and would grant him a few minutes before all hell broke loose.

"As you all know, with the recent trouble the family has had, there is a rat in house. Today, we eliminate him."

I pressed a button on the remote hidden in the pocket of my pants. Primed to play at the precise moment, Eva's pained voice filled the room, her confession that she was the rat spilling from the speakers. A roar sounded to my left. Frank launched himself at me, his hands going for my neck. Before he reached me, I yanked out my gun and shot him in both shoulders. He stumbled back. Blood seeped from his wounds. Dark stains grew around the injuries that even his black suit couldn't conceal.

"This proves nothing except you're a traitor!" Frank bellowed, his voice gravelly and filled with hate.

I kept my gun trained on him while exclamations of shock and outrage poured from the Sicilians. With my free hand, I withdrew the other holstered gun and leveled it at them. "I'm not done here." Their voices hushed, but anger simmered on their wrinkled faces.

Max unsheathed a knife and cut Tony loose. He stood and removed the gag from his mouth then sneered at Frank. But he remained quiet. It wasn't about him, at least not directly.

"Tony was bait, old man." I spat in Frank's direction as Marco wheeled Eva out from the office, strapped to the desk chair we'd tied her to. She struggled, screaming unintelligible words, no doubt pleading her case. But it was too late.

Frank pressed his mouth into a thin line. Before he could speak, I unloaded two shots to his chest and one to his head then turned and fired one into Eva's forehead. Frank dropped to his knees, blood sputtering from his mouth. All signs of life left his cold eyes as he crumpled to the ground. Eva's head had jerked back then listed to the side with a single hole in the center and a small trickle of blood leaking from the wound. A sense of freedom filled me as the life drained from Frank's body.

"What have you done?" the Sicilian boss, Mario Caruso, exclaimed.

I stared at Mario from behind my Glock. "I ended the threat to all our families." I rattled off the acts of betrayal, sticking to the main points only. "I'm stepping up as boss of the Rossi family," I said in a deep growl, "and *capo dei capi* to all the Chicago families, *capiche*?" I had just declared myself the boss of all bosses.

Enzo took a step toward me, and I shot him in the leg. He dropped to a knee then glared at me but didn't say a word. It was a clean shot. Through and through, merciful. He shouldn't have moved. It was a challenge to do so, and I had to prove myself in the eyes of the Sicilians—all of them.

"Anyone else?" Bloodlust raced through my veins, and I dared anyone to object.

Lorenzo Rossi stepped forward. "You've managed to uncover what none of us had. I have no objections." He swung his gaze to the others, and one by one, each of the bosses gave their consent. I'd had little dealings with the Sicilian Rossis and wasn't sure what to expect until he withdrew his saint's card, the one that would be bled on and burned to swear me in as boss. "Let's make this official."

CHAPTER TWENTY-ONE

EMILIANA

Two weeks later...

Laughter and the rich aroma of tomatoes, garlic, and red wine filled the dining room where I sat next to Stefano at our table. All the bosses and their wives or fiancées were present, including Sofia's brothers. The wine was passed around, and Stefano topped mine off. I looked around the table at everyone, and my heart warmed, even though my brother's hand tightened around his knife from time to time when he caught Stefano leaning close or resting his hand on my thigh. But Sofia always drew his focus back, forcing him to relax and accept that I'd made my choice to spend the rest of my life with Stefano.

Finally, nothing stood between Stefano and me. I was with my soul mate.

Stefano passed the bread, and I plucked a slice from the bowl before handing it to Sofia, the light hitting my wedding bands briefly, reminding me that everything I'd wanted, my dreams, had come true. And with everyone there, I felt complete.

Sofia, Lil, and I had a tradition of having a meal together at least once a week. In light of all the changes, Sunday dinner or occasionally breakfast was initiated at our house for the bosses and spouses of the Five Families.

We were surrounded by friends, and at the moment, we were united. Our bond, trust in each other, and loyalty made the Five Families stronger. But even with the newfound solidarity, changes were coming—I could feel it in my bones.

Stefano's hand found mine beneath the table, always in tune with my mood. We shared a quick look, and my heart swelled at the love shining in his eyes, the sheer determination and strength that made him a formidable leader and man. And I knew that he, too, sensed a shift in the family, in what we were becoming.

My gaze strayed to Lil. She had a half brother out there somewhere, something she'd told me in confidence. For the time being, in addition to his duties to the Caruso family, Max continued to oversee the Brambilla family with Vincenzo's blessing. Lil's brother was royalty by blood, though, and would eventually return to the fold. I couldn't help but wonder about the ripples his initiation would cause or the man he was.

I did a slow circle around the table, noting Trey's exhaustion that he tried to hide, but physically, the circles under his eyes told what his laughter did not. Nico joked with Trey. Sofia's brothers were fun, but Marco's glower worried me. Something was brewing and seemed to be connected to Max, given the way he'd growled at him earlier. I wondered when the rest of us would learn what was going on. I planned to ask Lil and Sofia when we had a moment to ourselves.

Tony wasn't there, but we were learning to trust him. In time, we would include him in our inner circle. Max would let us know when, as he was observing everything his half brother did with the clubs he managed. Without the pressure from Antonio, a new side to Tony was emerging. I wasn't holding my breath, but I would give him a chance.

I pursed my lips, leaning back against my chair. Stefano caught my gaze with his brows raised in a question. A slight shrug told him I wasn't sure what was up. I looked pointedly at Marco. Now and then, he would glare at Max. I wanted to know what was going on.

Sofia laughed, and I grinned at the way the joy-filled sound exploded amidst our easy banter. "Enz, you're going to have to step up your game. Em's lasagna is better than yours."

My brother snorted, and I couldn't help the grin from curving my mouth or the taunting words. "He was forever sneaking off to your house, Sof, skipping out on Mom's cooking lessons."

Heat stained her cheeks, and I tossed a piece of bread at my brother. "When are you going to marry Sofia? You've had the longest engagement out of all of us."

"I want a wedding like what you guys had. All those candles." She sighed, and Enzo smirked. It would be very soon if I knew my brother.

"How about this weekend, Sof?" Enzo tugged her close, throwing an arm around her shoulders. "Everyone is here. Let's take advantage of that before something changes." His gaze skimmed to Max and Lil before he focused back on the love of his life.

"I knew it!" I swiveled in my seat to face Lil and Max while Stefano's hand tightened on mine. "What's going on?"

Max rubbed a weary hand over the back of his neck. "Marco has agreed to bring Elena home."

Sofia's fork clattered to her plate, and the color leached from her face. "Remember, she's one of us, Marco."

But her brother didn't say a word. The only outward sign that he was affected was the clenching of his jaw and the muscle that twitched near his mouth. Worry pierced my consciousness. "We'll go. Sofia, Lil, and me. She'll come home if we're the ones that go to her."

"No." Stefano's voice boomed throughout the room. "The Pavlov Bratva is still a problem, and there is no way you'll put yourself at risk. Marco can handle it."

I narrowed my gaze at my husband. I knew that what he was saying was sound, but that didn't mean I liked it. He'd spoken with his sister Camila, who confirmed that Yuri planned retribution for his oldest son's death. We were on alert, but Marco… there had always been tension between Elena and him. I caught Sofia's gaze and registered that she, too, was wary of what would happen.

To keep the peace, I changed the subject. "How are you going to get a dress made by this Saturday, Sof?"

Trey grabbed the wine and poured himself another glass. "Please, she's been making them ever since Lil's impromptu wedding in anticipation of all of you getting married. I think she has, what is it"—he glanced at Nico then Enzo—"three almost-finished dresses?"

"Good." Lil clapped her hands once, a mischievous brightness entering her light eyes. "It's settled, then. This weekend you'll both make it official because of all this living in sin—"

Nico snorted then coughed in his hand. "Mafia."

Sofia snickered, but Lil soldiered on, "Whatever. I, for one, am looking forward to another wedding."

"Me too." I turned to Stefano and sucked in a breath at the desire reflected in his dark gaze. He'd been watching me during the exchange. Heat spread through me, and I felt my body soften, my skin instantly hyperaware in anticipation of his touch. While I loved our family, I suddenly wanted them all gone and his hands on me.

In the distance, I registered Enzo growling and Sofia

smacking him on the arm as she reprimanded him with, "They're married."

It didn't take long for the dishes to be cleared and the night to come to a close. I couldn't help but dwell on the imminent war with the Russians or the changes that would unfold next month. But whatever life threw at us, I knew we would handle it. As soon as the elevator left with all of them, Stefano pulled me into his arms, and his mouth covered mine in a toe-curling kiss. I would never tire of him. Each time felt as if it was the first. He was the other half of my soul and my best friend. That was my last thought as I sank into his embrace and desire infused my blood. The room faded until it was only the two of us.

"Let me love you, Em."

My arms tightened around the fierce man who held me as I whispered a heated yes. I had always been his.

The End

Continue reading the Mafia Elite series with SAVAGE SECRETS:
https://amymckinleyauthor.com/mafia-elite/

If you enjoyed reading BORN IN DARKNESS as much as I did writing it, I hope you'll consider leaving a review.

SAVAGE SECRETS

RELEASING JANUARY 2022

Chicago Mafia boss Marco La Rosa thought the only woman he'd ever loved had died years ago. But when her brother approaches him with an arranged marriage contract, he learns that she is very much alive and in danger. Bringing her back within the fold of the Five Families is a second chance he can't pass up. The only problem is, he has to get to her before their enemies do.

On-the-run Mafia princess Elena Caruso cut all family ties to survive. She knows that the Bratva is on her tail and that someday they'll find her. When she receives word that her cover's blown, she attempts to flee. But it isn't the Russians who get to her first. It's the boy she's been in love with for years, who's now a dangerous and devastatingly handsome man—and she's running from him too.

As threats quickly close in, her only chance for survival is into the arms of the Mafia boss who once held her heart.

Continue reading the Mafia Elite series with SAVAGE
SECRETS:
https://amymckinleyauthor.com/mafia-elite/

ACKNOWLEDGMENTS

I couldn't do this without my family—huge thank you to my husband and four kids, who are amazing. I'm very fortunate to have their support.

Candice Irvin, thank you so much for jumping in when I was beyond exhausted. I cannot thank you enough for your willingness to brainstorm or read over sections at a moment's notice. I value your creative input.

Emily Albright and Kristin Kisska, thank you for the hours of reading all my books when they aren't on an insane deadline and I run out of time. But even when that happens, you both have been there for me each step of the way. I am beyond grateful for your support and encouragement. I'm thankful to have them in my inner circle.

I have an incredible team of editors. Taylor Anhalt always has a significant role in the development of my books. I loved her content edit and how she helped to shape this story into what it is today. I have a fabulous team from Red Adept Editing. Kate Birdsall has been editing for me for the past several years. She helps to make my stories better and gets my thought process. Working with her is so much fun.

As always, I'm thrilled with the cover design by T.E. Black Designs. No matter the genre, she understands my vision and can match that with the genre's vibe. As always, each project exceeds my expectations.

I'm grateful to have Danielle Sanchez with Wildfire Marketing Solutions and Colleen Noyes with Itsy Bitsy Book Bits in my corner working their magic to make each release a success.

Last but certainly not least, a special thank you to all the bloggers and readers who have encouraged and helped me along the way and who continue to make my dream a reality.

Thank you.

ABOUT THE AUTHOR

Amy McKinley is the *USA Today* best-selling author of the romantic suspense thriller Gray Ghost Novels, Deadly Isles Special Ops, Covert Recruits, Mafia Elite, Moonlit Destination Series, the Five Fates paranormal romance books, and several standalone titles. Her edge-of-your-seat books are filled with surprising twists and just the right amount of heat and danger. She lives in Illinois with her husband, two daughters, two sons, and three mischievous cats.

You can find her at: www.AmyMcKinley.com

Subscribe to Amy's newsletter for book announcements: http://eepurl.com/dEBqJn

goodreads.com/amymckinley_author
bookbub.com/authors/amy-mckinley
facebook.com/amymckinleyauthor
instagram.com/amymckinleyauthor

Irina

Sasha

Zena

Nadia

Katya

-

Standalone Titles

Shattered Melody

Siren's Call: Cursed Seas

Fake Fiancé (A Second Chance Office Romance)

-

Moonlit Destination Series

Moonlit Whisper

Moonlit Kiss

Moonlit Mirage

Five Fates Series

Hidden

Taken

www.ingramcontent.com/pod-product-compliance
Lightning Source LLC
Chambersburg PA
CBHW062310200726
48292CB00004BA/1494